ENDANGERED
ANIMALS

RANGER RICK ✿ BOOKS
PUBLISHED BY THE NATIONAL WILDLIFE FEDERATION

Library of Congress CIP Data: page 95.

ENDANGERED
ANIMALS

Can you imagine never seeing a bird soar in a blue sky, a bumblebee buzz from blossom to blossom, or a raccoon scamper across the road?

Many of us take for granted that we will always have animals around to enjoy as our friends and companions, to help us with our work, or to provide food. But you will learn in this book that even though humans are the most intelligent of all animals, we have done unwise things that have hurt other animals who also call Earth home.

Every day, the National Wildlife Federation reminds people that we must look at the Earth as a big neighborhood, and we must take care not to destroy the homes of our animal neighbors.

After all, many animals were living on some blocks of this neighborhood long before humans came along. Sadly, some of those animals have already disappeared forever, because humans took away or damaged their homes. We call animals' homes—which can be forests or oceans, swamps or mountains—their habitat.

The National Wildlife Federation works to protect animals' natural homes from being polluted or destroyed by humans.

For example, the Federation asked the government to stop farmers from using certain poisons on crops to kill insects, be-cause the poisons also kill many animals, like the bald eagle. The great bald eagle, the symbol of our country, might have been gone forever, just like the dinosaur, if groups like the Federation had not been here to make sure it was protected.

We have asked the government to make sure scientists and biologists have enough money to do research about animals, to discover if humans are hurting them, and to find ways to correct harm already done.

We have also asked the government to make it illegal for humans to pollute or destroy animals' homes.

The Federation teaches people all over the world about the importance of animals

in making the neighborhood a good place for everyone to live. Not only do we enjoy seeing birds fly and sing, we depend on animals for many needs.

By being a good neighbor on this planet Earth, we will have the time to get to know all our wildlife neighbors and discover how we can help one another.

Jay D. Hair

Jay D. Hair, President
National Wildlife Federation

CONTENTS

2

1

GONE FOREVER?

News reports from around the world all tell the same story. Animals and plants of many different kinds are disappearing. In the 1800s, pioneers marveled as millions of bison grazed and stampeded across the western plains of the United States. Today, only a few thousand of the animals survive on protected parklands. No wild gray wolves have been seen in England in more than 200 years. And in Africa, the number of black rhinos has dropped from 65,000 in 1970 to only 4,000 in 1986. What on earth is going on? Is the disappearance of all these creatures something new? Let's see.

Life on earth is always changing. For millions of years, large dinosaurs and small dinosaurs, plant-eaters and meat-eaters, roamed across the land. Flying reptiles ruled the skies and strange swimming creatures called plesiosaurs and ichthyosaurs lived in the seas. Today, all of these animals are gone. They are *extinct.* That means that not one of them can be found anywhere on earth.

About 40 million years ago, tiny horses no larger than foxes trotted across the western plains. Today, only the fossil bones of the little horse known as Eohippus remain. This animal is extinct, too.

It seems a shame that these animals aren't around. They would be fascinating to watch. But their extinction was natural. Some species, or kinds, of animals died out

3   4

How is a dinosaur like a dusky sea-side sparrow? Both are extinct. Natural events wiped out the dinosaur (1), but dusky seaside sparrows (2) died out when people drained the Florida swamps where the birds lived. Such loss of habitat threatens many other animals, from Indonesia's orangutan (3) to Florida's key deer (4).

and other species eventually took their place. Some of the dinosaurs were giant plant eaters that lived in hot, dry places. Today we have elephants. They are also giant plant eaters, and some elephants live in hot, dry places. If we still had dinosaurs we might not have elephants.

Since extinction is natural, why should people be concerned about it? Because today a new kind of extinction is taking place, one that is not natural. This new extinction is caused by people, and we call the creatures that are in danger of disappearing *endangered* animals.

The dodo (1), a large, flightless bird, might have been raised to provide food for hungry nations. But the bird was extinct by the 17th century.

Flocks of millions of passenger pigeons (3), which darkened skies in the early 18th century, died out because their forest homes were cut down and the remaining birds were overhunted by pioneers moving west. The only passenger pigeons left today are stuffed pigeons in museums (2).

Herds of bison survive in the American West, but in far smaller numbers than those seen by Indians and early settlers (4).

It's already too late for some animals. Dodos were turkey-sized birds that lived on the island of Mauritius in the Indian Ocean. When European explorers first landed there in 1507, they found the birds very tasty. Dodos were easy to catch, too, since they could not fly at all and didn't run very fast. By 1681, all the dodos were gone. Like the dinosaurs, they became extinct—but their extinction was caused by people, not nature.

As recently as the 1800s, the sky over parts of North America turned dark when flocks of billions of passenger pigeons passed overhead. But people cut down the

The Dodo.

Geo Edwards, Sculp. A.D. 1759.

1

forests where the birds lived and killed the birds faster than they could replace their lost numbers. Finally, in 1914, the world's last passenger pigeon died in a zoo.

Some scientists like to compare the earth to a giant airplane. They say the earth's different plants and creatures are like the rivets that hold the airplane together. If enough rivets are lost, the airplane will fall apart. If enough plants and creatures are lost, life for the animals that are left could be in danger.

Why could this happen? Because people and wildlife and plants really depend on each other. In Southeast Asia, for example, the durian is a strange-tasting fruit that many people enjoy eating. But durian trees are pollinated almost entirely by one kind of bat. Without pollination, the trees cannot grow fruit. A few years ago, people started cleaning out the caves where these bats lived, and many bats died. Soon, the supply of durian fruit began to decline. Luckily, some bats survived in nearby forests. But if something happens and these bats also die, the people may lose a popular food.

What if the endangered animal is dangerous? Should we care if a species that hurts people dies off? Yes, we should. Look at cobras, for example. Every year, cobras kill

2

3

4

Taking the animals and their eggs for food has endangered sea turtles.

people in India. But at the same time, these snakes eat a lot of rats that would otherwise eat the people's corn and other foods. What about killing all the rats? That might solve one problem, but rats are also very useful. Rats often react to foods and poisons the way people do, so doctors use them for testing to make sure new food additives and medicines are safe. Rats are also an important food for birds of prey and other animals.

When scientists say that a species is endangered, they are raising a warning flag. They are telling us that something is going wrong. Otherwise the animals would not be

DDT sprayed to protect crops hurt eagles and other birds by causing them to lay eggs with shells that crushed too easily.

Clearing the jungle destroys the homes of many animals. Brazil's golden lion tamarin has almost disappeared.

in trouble. We need to find out why the species is disappearing and what can be done about it.

Maybe people are killing the animals faster than new animals are born to replace them. At one time, that was happening to deer in the eastern United States. Hunting limits were set, and now some states have more than 500 times as many deer as they did at the turn of the century.

Poisons in the environment may also be killing the animals or hurting their young. In the 1960s, a famous writer named Rachel Carson warned everyone that the country faced a "silent spring," a time when no birds would be around to sing in the springtime. Birds were eating food contaminated with DDT, a powerful chemical people used to kill insect pests. Once they ate this poison,

the birds were unable to lay eggs with thick shells. Their thin-shelled eggs easily collapsed and the baby birds inside died. Luckily, enough people listened to the warning and passed laws to control the use of DDT so it wouldn't harm wildlife.

The leading cause of endangerment and extinction today is loss of habitat. Animals are running out of places to find food and raise their young. Many kinds of animals—and plants—are endangered. They live in all parts of the world. Starting on the next page, you will learn about just a few of the most interesting creatures that are in danger of becoming extinct. The United States government names more than 800 animals in its list of endangered and threatened wildlife. But many more are probably in trouble, including creatures that we don't even know about.

GIANT PANDA

People love giant pandas. These 250-pound animals from China look like overgrown, roly-poly teddy bears. Any zoo that has pandas can count on crowds of children and grownups coming to see them.

The first live panda arrived in the United States in the 1930s. That animal, named Su-Lin, was an immediate sensation. People came from all over the world to see her. She got more news coverage than almost any person of her day. When Su-Lin died, zoo officials found out that "she" was really a "he."

But just liking giant pandas is not enough to save them from extinction. A million years ago, these animals ranged throughout eastern China and into Burma. Now, only a few small groups are left in central China. Every day these few face the threats of poaching, starvation, and loss of places to live and raise their young. Today, scientists from many nations are studying how pandas live in order to develop ways to protect them.

Studying pandas is hard work. The bamboo thickets where the animals live hide them from friends as well as from enemies. One scientist in China went out every day to study pandas, but he found them only about once a month.

Even when scientists find pandas, they have trouble following them on the steep mountainsides and through the thickets. The pandas normally stay in high mountains, usually above 8,000 feet. That's higher than any mountain in the eastern United States.

People who live near the pandas report seeing a few of them every now and then. One time, a farmer spotted a panda among the sheep he was herding. The panda quietly followed the sheep into their enclosure and spent the night with them.

At least one Chinese naturalist finds all the trouble worthwhile. "There are some young people who would like to learn more about the giant panda," he says. "But, most of them get tired of such a difficult life. Luckily, I find happiness in hardship!"

Scientists used to wonder what kind of animal the panda really is. People often call it a "panda bear." The latest tests show that inside, a panda *is* like a bear. But it is also very much like a raccoon. One panda expert says simply, "The panda is a panda."

Unlike bears, pandas don't hibernate in the winter. Instead, they move downhill a few thousand feet to find warmer weather. Unless it wanders far away looking for more

Pandas live in mountainous bamboo forests, where they spend about two-thirds of their time feeding. In just one day, a panda eats up to 40 pounds of leafy bamboo stems. When the bamboo in an area dies out, the pandas are in danger of starving.

food or for a mate, a panda stays in the high mountains the rest of the year.

Panda mothers raise one cub every two or three years. The newborn pandas are really tiny. It would take 30 of them to weigh as much as a human baby. Their eyes stay shut for about two months and they stay with their mother for about half a year. It takes another five or six years for them to grow up. By then they weigh 150 to 350 pounds.

How long do pandas live? We don't know about wild ones, but pandas in captivity live as long as 30 years.

Though they look cute, cuddly, and slow, pandas are really strong and fast. And with their sharp claws and strong jaws, they can be dangerous. One zoo keeper forgot to be careful, and an angry panda bit off his hand. "We baby and spoil them when they are young," the man said. "Then as they mature they get too strong for a man to handle. And as we become more and more reluctant to play with them, they miss the attention and get bad tempered."

Pandas seem most content when they sit and nibble on bamboo leaves and stems. They have a "sixth finger," which is really a thumblike bone that sticks out from their wristbone. This extra finger helps them handle bamboo more easily. They sometimes eat other plants and even fish. But their main food is bamboo, up to 40 pounds a day.

As long as the pandas can get enough bamboo, they are all right. But bamboo is a strange plant. It is really a giant grass. Every 40 years or so, all the bamboo in an area dies out. In the past, pandas survived by moving up or down the mountainsides to find other kinds of bamboo that hadn't died. But today, those mountainsides have often been cleared for farmland, leaving only one kind of bamboo. When that kind dies out as part of its natural cycle, the pandas have nothing left to eat and they may die, too.

In 1983, the Chinese were ready when the bamboo started to die. Rescue teams found the pandas and carried them to places where bamboo was still growing. Even with this effort, some pandas still didn't survive.

Poaching—taking animals illegally—is another problem for pandas. Sometimes the animals are accidentally killed in traps set by poachers to catch valuable musk deer. And sometimes the poachers are after the pandas. Panda skins are worth $100,000 each in some parts of the world.

Can the panda be saved? Scientists say yes, but it won't be easy. In 1963, zoo keepers in Beijing, China, succeeded in breeding pandas in captivity for the first time. Other zoos have tried over the years, but many times the newborn animals do not survive.

Every effort to raise new pandas helps. But experts agree that the best hope is to protect the animals in their mountain homes. Luckily, the Chinese consider pandas important and are trying hard to save them.

Baby pandas, like this six-month-old (above), are rare. A panda mother raises only one cub at a time in the wild, and it often dies before maturing. People hoped that captive pandas (left) would breed. But few panda youngsters born in zoos have survived.

WHOOPING CRANE

Scientist Ernie Kuyt is an egg thief. Each spring he sneaks up to whooping crane nests in Wood Buffalo National Park, Canada, and takes an egg from each nest.

Kuyt is not a real thief. He doesn't keep the eggs for himself, and he means the cranes no harm. In fact, he is doing everything he can to save this endangered bird. He carefully places the eggs in heated suitcases lined with foam. Then he carries them to a nesting site in Idaho, hundreds of miles away. There, he takes the eggs from the nests of another bird, the more common sandhill crane. He replaces them with whooping crane eggs.

With the help of an unusual "foster parent" program, the rare whooping crane is making a comeback. Scientists put extra whooper eggs into sandhill crane nests (inset) to be hatched and raised by the foster parents. The sandhills don't seem to notice that their rusty-white adopted chick is unusually large (above).

What's the reason for the switch? Whooping cranes, the tallest birds in America, are also one of the rarest birds in the world. They lay two eggs each spring, but usually raise only one chick. In 1967, scientists designed an experiment. They wanted to see if whooping crane eggs could be hatched artificially in incubators. They also wanted to see if captive sandhill cranes would raise the whoopers as their own. Both parts of the experiment succeeded.

More recently, scientists took this experiment a step further. If sandhills could raise whoopers in captivity, the scientists reasoned, why couldn't they hatch and raise whoopers in the wild? So far, hundreds of whooper eggs have been carried from Canada to be raised by sandhills in Idaho. More than 170 eggs have hatched. Some of the chicks were eaten by coyotes and other predators. Others died when they flew into power lines. But at least 14 of these birds are alive today.

At nearly five feet tall, the whooping crane towers over most children. When a whooper flies, its wings spread seven feet from tip to tip.

Until the mid-1800s, about 1,400 whoopers lived in isolated, open, marshy areas throughout North America. A flock of whoopers takes up a lot of space. Each pair needs three or four hundred acres of territory, a special area where the birds hunt for food. If other cranes come into this territory, the pair chases them away.

As settlers moved westward, people took over the prairies where the whooping cranes lived. Farmers drained the swamps and plowed the fields. People shot the birds for food, and egg collectors robbed their nests.

A newly hatched whooper chick stays near the nest (inset) for less than a week, eating food delivered by its parents. By the time it is ready to fly south, it will be right alongside the adults (above) catching crabs, frogs, and water insects.

By 1910, the world's population of whooping cranes had been almost wiped out.

By 1941, only 16 migrating whooping cranes were left. These birds arrived each winter in a Texas coastal swamp known as Aransas. To save these last cranes, the federal government bought Aransas and made it a National Wildlife Refuge. Now the birds were safe for the winter. But in spring, they left Texas to nest and to hatch their chicks. No one knew where their nesting place was. Scientists worried that if they couldn't find and save the cranes' nesting area, it would be destroyed, and the cranes would die out.

One scientist, Robert Allen, was assigned to watch the birds and to find their hidden nesting spot. Allen spent many winters in Aransas and summers in Canada. But he never found the nesting area.

In 1954, a Canadian forester spotted the nesting area in a secluded section of a Canadian park, about 2,500 miles from the birds' winter range in Texas. Perhaps the birds owe their survival to the fact that their nests were in a protected park area.

When they reach their nesting site in Canada, the females lay their eggs. The chicks hatch in about 30 days. Young whoopers are only four months old when they accompany their parents on the fall migration to Texas. Scientists tracking whooping cranes have timed them at more than 35 miles per hour. The birds stop and feed along the way, so the journey between Canada and Texas takes a month.

In Texas, the young bird first trails after its parents, and they often feed it. Whooping cranes eat crabs, frogs, minnows, or insects that they pull out of the water. Both the adult and the young birds also feed on grains and berries that they find on land.

As spring nears, the parents become more interested in each other than in the young bird. Together they perform a ballet-like dance to show they are ready to mate again. They leap into the air, madly nodding their long necks. Or they stretch their necks to the sky and trumpet the whooping noise that gives them their name. The youngster, left out of this ritual, begins to find its own food. But when the birds fly back to Canada, the entire family flies side by side.

Each year, Robert Allen watched the family cycle of the whooping crane repeat itself. Each year, he counted the number of cranes. The count climbed very slowly at first. New cranes were born in Canada each year. But, each year during migration, some cranes were shot by irresponsible hunters. Others were caught and eaten by hungry animals.

Robert Allen is gone now, but scientists still count the number of whooping cranes returning to Aransas. By 1988, the number had reached nearly 200. That's almost ten times the number of birds 50 years ago.

Male and female whooping cranes lift their heads together in a display that strengthens the bond between the two birds. They also perform a "dance," jumping up and down and tossing sticks and grass into the air.

HUMPBACK WHALE

People have hunted whales on the high seas for a thousand years. Whale oil was burned in lamps and used to make soap, wax, and other products. The bones were ground up to make glue and fertilizer.

Humpback whales sometimes flop their 35-ton bodies out of the water in an action known as breaching. No one knows for sure why whales breach. Maybe they are trying to shake off tiny animals called barnacles that attach themselves to the whales. Some humpbacks carry 1,000 pounds of barnacles.

The meat was used to feed people and animals. But over the years, whalers found fewer and fewer animals to catch. Whalers had to design faster ships to chase their prey and deadlier weapons to kill them.

Humpbacks were popular among whalers because they are easy to catch. They swim slowly. During breeding season, they stay close to shore. And they often swim toward ships instead of away from them. In the early 1900s, whalers near Antarctica easily captured humpbacks by the hundreds. As soon as a whale was dead, it was pumped full of air so it would float. The ship would return later to pick it up.

Whaling cut the world's population of humpback whales from more than 100,000 to about 6,000. Whaling was dangerous for the whalers, too. Crewmen like these had to row right up to the harpooned whale so an officer could kill the whale with his lance.

Sometimes, the whalers found it easier to kill more than they needed rather than try to find all the dead whales they had left floating. As a result, one out of every three or four humpbacks killed was never used. This waste just made matters worse for the humpbacks. At one time, the oceans held more than 100,000 humpbacks. By the 1960s, that figure had dropped to only about 6,000. Only then did people outlaw harvesting of humpback whales. It was almost too late. Nearly 95 percent of the humpbacks were gone.

Humpbacks belong to a group of whales known as the baleen whales. They don't have teeth. Instead, they have rows of filters, called baleen, that strain shrimp and other small creatures from sea water. As its mouth fills with water and food, a humpback's throat expands like an accordion. Then the whale squeezes the water out through the baleen and swallows the food left behind.

Humpbacks also herd shrimp and other small creatures close together to make catching them easier. First, the whale swims in circles under them and blows out a stream of bubbles that rises around them. Blocked by bubbles on all sides, the creatures crowd together. Then, with its mouth wide open, the whale swims up through them and takes in a big mouthful.

Humpbacks grow quite large on their seafood diet. An average humpback is about 40 feet long and weighs 35 tons. That's as long as three large cars sitting end to end —and as heavy as five or six elephants.

Although they are large, humpbacks and other whales are good swimmers. Humpbacks normally don't go very fast, though —only about the speed of a person walking.

Whales' streamlined shapes allow them to move easily through the water. Their heads are stretched out, with no neck or shoulders to interrupt the smooth flow of water around their bodies. Their ears are two small openings on the side of the head. The only parts that stick out are a pair of fins or flippers, a tiny back fin, and a wide tail.

This tail is powered by huge muscles in the whale's back. The tail acts like a skindiver's flippers to drive the whale through the water. Whales sometimes make noise by

Huge tails, measuring 12 feet or so across, propel humpback whales through the water at about four miles per hour. In summer, some of the whales move to the coast of Alaska (top right), where they feed together on shrimp and other small sea creatures. The whales may use their noisy "songs" to help herd together their tiny prey. In winter, humpbacks move to warmer waters where the females bear one youngster (left) every two years.

slamming their tails down on the water's surface. This may be one way the whales send signals to each other.

Humpbacks and other whales often swim in water that is close to freezing. Still, they stay warm on the inside. They keep their body temperature about the same as a human's. How? One way is by keeping on the move. Whales swim almost all the time and sleep only in short naps.

Whales are also insulated from the cold by a layer of fat just under their skin. This fat, called blubber, measures nearly two feet thick in some kinds of whales. Blubber isn't soft like the fat on bacon. Instead, it is filled with fibers and is as tough as bacon rind.

Sometimes whales need to lose heat, not keep it in. That often happens when the whales are chasing fast-moving prey in warm water. Then the whales' flippers and tail act as radiators. Flippers and tails have little blubber, so blood pumped through them cools off quickly. Water carries off the heat much faster than air does.

Humpbacks spend the winter breeding season in the waters around Bermuda and Hawaii. The whales apparently return to the same sites from year to year. There the males push and shove each other to get close to the females. Now the whales are not gentle giants, and they sometimes bump each other hard enough to draw blood.

About a year after mating, the female gives birth to a single youngster, called a calf. Anywhere from 6 to 12 years later, this new whale is ready to have youngsters of its own. Like many people, it lives into its 70s.

People today are taking a new interest in humpbacks—not to kill them for their meat and oil but to watch them and listen to their unusual "songs."

Humpback's songs aren't tunes with toe-tapping rhythms. They often sound more like snores, groans, chirps, or even screams. But they do have patterns. Whales in different breeding grounds sing different songs, but all the humpbacks in one area sing in the same pattern. Scientists with special underwater listening equipment have heard humpback songs from 100 miles away.

Only male humpbacks sing, and then only when they are in their winter breeding grounds. Why do they sing? Scientists aren't sure. The males may be trying to attract mates, locate other members of their group, or warn other males to stay away.

Besides their songs, humpbacks are known for their spectacular leaps out of the water. This behavior is called breaching, and most kinds of whales do it. Why? This is another puzzle for scientists to figure out.

The whales may be trying to shake off barnacles—although whales that don't have barnacles breach, too. Maybe one whale is showing another which animal is boss. Maybe the whale is trying to stun small fish so it can catch them. And maybe the whale is jumping for fun. Now that humpbacks are no longer hunted, their numbers may be increasing in some places. You might say that they have good reason to jump for joy.

ENDANGERED WHALES

1. GRAY WHALE
2. RIGHT WHALE

For centuries, whalers killed as many whales as they could. Whales provided food, oil, and other products. Although some countries agreed in the 1930s not to hunt certain species, other nations refused to go along. Finally, by the 1980s, all but a few countries had stopped whaling. Luckily, no whales have been hunted to extinction, but many are endangered. Most of these endangered animals are baleen whales, the toothless kinds that filter their food from the water. The only endangered toothed whale is the sperm whale, whose high-quality oil was once used to lubricate expensive tools.

3. BLUE WHALE

4. MINKE WHALE

5. SPERM WHALE

6. FIN WHALE

7. SEI WHALE

In September of 1981, a Wyoming rancher's dog brought home a strange animal in its jaws. The dog was carrying a skinny, tan-colored animal that was about 1½ feet long and had a creamy white stomach. A dark brown mask like a raccoon's marked its eyes.

The rancher was curious. He tried to find someone to identify the dead animal. Eventually, a group of excited scientists confirmed that the creature was a black-footed ferret, one of the rarest animals in America.

For almost ten years, scientists had believed that these ferrets were extinct.

Could more ferrets be living somewhere nearby? The scientists said yes, and they knew just where to look. They knew because they understood the ferret's feeding habits.

Black-footed ferrets mainly eat squirrel-sized animals called prairie dogs. Large colonies of prairie dogs live in underground dens joined by tunnels. Unfortunately for the prairie dogs, black-footed ferrets live in these same tunnels. The ferrets are the right shape to slither easily through the tunnels. When a ferret finds a prairie dog, it kills and eats it.

To look for black-footed ferrets, the scientists first found a colony of prairie dogs. That was easy. Mounds of dirt dotting open fields marked the openings to their underground homes. But finding the ferrets was not easy. Ferrets hunt mostly at night and sleep underground during the day. The scientists stayed up all night for many nights, waiting and watching with powerful searchlights. It took two months to spot a tiny ferret's head bobbing from a hole.

In spite of temperatures below zero, the scientists worked all through the Wyoming winter. After snow fell, the search for more ferrets became easier. Ferret tracks show up well in the snow. By spring, the researchers had counted 22 ferrets. After new litters were born that spring, the ferret population was estimated to be more than 60 animals.

As the population of ferrets grew, researchers were able to learn more about the behavior of this rare little animal. Although ferrets eat mostly prairie dogs, they sometimes feed on mice and other small animals.

One study showed that a ferret travels up to four miles a night in search of dinner.

BLACK-FOOTED FERRET

Black-footed ferrets are just the right shape to slither through prairie dog tunnels (opposite). These ferrets, now probably extinct in the wild, lived in the tunnels and fed on the prairie dogs.

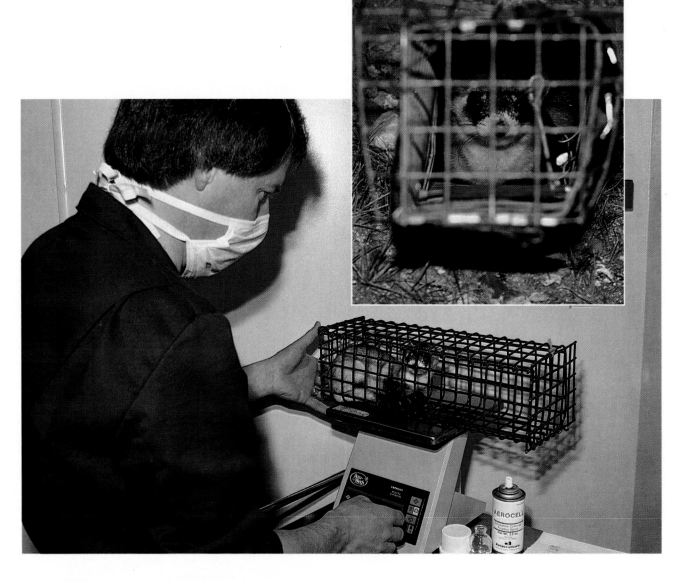

When disease almost wiped out the last black-footed ferrets, scientists captured the survivors and brought them to a safe lab (above). There, people hope to breed a new colony that can be returned to the wild (opposite).

Ferrets normally live and hunt alone, and each one probably marks its own hunting territory with a special smell. To a ferret on the prowl, this scent serves as a "no trespassing" sign. When one ferret comes across another's scent, it knows to keep out.

A mother ferret has to hunt extra hard. From about May to August, she must feed herself *and* her babies. The babies, usually numbering three or four, stay in their underground dens for about a month. Then the mother brings them above ground, moving them to different dens every few nights. By the end of August, the mother separates the babies, leaving each one in a different den. Soon, they learn to fend for themselves.

Unfortunately, the scientists saw only a few new litters of ferrets. During the next three years, no new ferrets were seen. The scientists' hope and excitement came to an

early end. In l985, this last-known group of black-footed ferrets on earth began dying. They died from distemper, a disease carried by many animals.

Worried scientists captured as many of the animals as they could. They hoped to keep the species alive by breeding the remaining ferrets in captivity. On March 1, 1987, scientists caught the last known ferret left in the wild.

In l988 in a Wyoming laboratory, the captive female ferrets gave birth to a total of 44 youngsters. If the number of ferrets reaches about 300, they will be set free. With help, these ferrets may someday be able to start a new population in the wild.

If these creatures survive, it will be the first good news for black-footed ferrets since the pioneers moved westward more than 100 years ago. In those days, an estimated five

billion prairie dogs lived in prairie dog towns covering thousands of acres. Ranchers saw the prairie dogs as pests that ate crops and dug holes that cattle stepped into, breaking their legs. Ranchers poisoned and shot prairie dogs and plowed through their towns.

Only one percent of the original prairie dog population has survived. Black-footed ferrets, who live mostly on prairie dogs, were always more scarce than their prey. As the prairie dogs died off, so did the ferrets.

Could more ferrets be out there hiding in some deep prairie dog tunnel? No one knows for sure. In l988, the New York Zoological Society posted a $5,000 reward for anyone finding a live one. Even if a few more ferrets turn up somewhere, their future is still in doubt. The only real hope for the species' survival probably lies in that laboratory in Wyoming.

KOMODO DRAGON

Fairy tales tell of gallant knights fighting fire-breathing dragons to save damsels in distress. Today, the story is just the other way around. Real-life Komodo dragons are the ones in trouble.

Komodo dragons are giant reptiles. They live on the island of Komodo and a few other isolated spots in the Southeast Asian country of Indonesia. Until the early part of this century, no one except a few traders and fishermen had actually seen the dragons. These early observers brought back tales of monstrous creatures that had forked tongues and climbed trees and attacked people. The animals certainly sounded like dragons.

Then in 1912, scientists decided to go to Komodo to see just what these dragons were really like. Komodo is a small volcanic island only 12 miles wide and 22 miles long. One explorer called it "a lost world." Getting there is not easy. Powerful winds and currents make the trip by boat very difficult.

Landing on Komodo Island is only half the problem. The other half is capturing a live dragon. One group of scientists hoped to attract a hungry dragon by baiting a trap with a dead goat. What they found out was that dragons want their dead prey to be really rotten. By the time a dragon entered the trap, the smell was so bad the scientists could hardly stand to get near it. Their problems weren't over, either. The first dragon they caught later chewed its way through the steel wire around the trap and got away.

When the scientists finally examined a live dragon, they discovered that it was really a giant monitor lizard. Some other monitor lizards measure barely eight inches long. The largest Komodo dragon measured ten feet and weighed 365 pounds.

Except for their size, all monitor lizards look pretty much alike. They have long heads and necks, heavy bodies, and long, thick tails. Like snakes, monitors have forked tongues that pick up the scent of their prey. Their strong legs hold them well off the ground when they walk. And their sharp claws make dangerous weapons.

Why are these lizards called monitors? There are at least two stories about that. One says that the lizards act as monitors and give a warning when dangerous crocodiles come around. More believable is the report that a scientist reading a report in a foreign language translated the name wrong.

Like other monitors, Komodo dragons are meat eaters. It doesn't matter if their meal is dead or alive. They hunt the way large cats do. They wait in ambush and pounce on deer, wild pigs, and other island creatures. When a likely meal passes by, a hungry dragon jumps, grabs the animal by the leg or throat, and throws it to the ground. A Komodo's appetite is enormous. A 100-pound dragon once ate a 90-pound wild pig—legs, hoofs, and all.

Now the dragons themselves are in danger. No one kills Komodo dragons for food or hunts them for their hides. In fact, no one is allowed to hurt the dragons. People are not taking over their homes, either. But the animals are endangered anyway. Why? Because so few of them are left and they live in only a few places. It wouldn't take much—a terrible storm, a volcanic eruption, a deadly disease—to wipe them all out. Komodo and the other islands probably never held more than about 7,000 dragons. That's not many when you remember that Pennsylvania alone has more than a million white-tailed deer.

The giant Komodo dragon is a fearsome sight, even when it's resting. This lizard grows up to 10 feet long and is covered with tough, clay-colored scales. The Komodo dragon uses its powerful front legs and long claws to climb over rocks and pin down its prey when feeding. When not feeding, the lizard looks for shady places where it can sleep. Its body is close to the ground, where temperatures reach 165° F during the hottest part of the day.

TIGER

Largest of all cats, a prowling tiger is a frightening sight. It normally hunts pigs, deer, antelope, and buffalo.

Should we save the tiger? The answer is not as simple as you might think. Yes, the tiger is a beautiful animal. Like any creature, it deserves to live, free and undisturbed. But what happens when the needs of animals and the needs of people clash? Usually the animal is the loser. The problem is how to make sure that both people and tigers can win.

People in India and other countries where tigers live have mixed feelings about the animals. They know that tigers are endangered and that they attract tourists the countries need to make money. They also recognize how strong and beautiful tigers are. But its strength and beauty also make the animal a prize target for collectors. Just one skin good enough to use for a rug or wall hanging can be sold for up to $2,000. And people also know that tigers threaten their livestock and even the people themselves. Hungry tigers on the prowl make deadly enemies.

Tigers are the largest cats in the world. Siberian tigers, which roam the northern forests of eastern Russia, grow to be the largest tigers of all. An adult male weighs more than 600 pounds and measures about ten feet in length. Two or three feet of this length is its tail. The female Siberian is a bit smaller.

If you look at newborn tiger cubs, it's hard to believe the animals grow so big. A cub weighs half as much as a human baby.

From two to four cubs are born at a time. Their mother hides them in the shelter of tall grass, rocks, or caves. Like newborn kittens, tiger cubs are born with their eyes and ears closed, but they open within a week or two. In only two months, the cubs are ready to follow their mother when she goes hunting.

Tigers have three or four cubs, but often only one or two survive. The others die from disease or animal attacks, possibly by jackals and adult male tigers.

All tigers are hunters. They are built to bring down large prey. Their toes have sharp, curved claws up to four inches long. Their fangs are almost as long. Like housecats, tigers keep their claws drawn back into their paws until they need them for catching prey or defending themselves. The main function of their teeth is to help kill prey.

Unlike housecats, tigers like water and can swim well. Most easily cross rivers five miles wide—and one tiger was seen still swimming after going more than 15 miles.

Most tigers hunt in the same area, or home range, from year to year. How large a range a tiger needs depends on how much food it can find. In parts of India, a tiger may need only 25 square miles to live in. That's about twice the size of Manhattan Island in New York City. In China, some tigers cover areas about as large as the state of Connecticut. But a few tigers don't bother with home ranges at all. They go anywhere they can find enough to eat.

A hungry tiger can eat 40 to 80 pounds of meat in one meal. To get enough to eat, a tiger normally preys on large mammals such as wild boar, deer, moose, and Indian buf-

Tigers drag their prey to a quiet spot where other animals cannot find it. Later, they may spend the entire night eating. When the prey is large, a hungry tiger stuffs itself so full it can barely stand.

falo. A really hungry tiger will hunt almost any animal, from a peacock or frog to a crocodile or dog.

Catching large or fast prey is not easy. A tiger may have to chase 20 different animals before it finally brings one down. Tigers are not built for chasing prey over long distances. Instead, they stalk their prey. They move in slowly and quietly from the side or back where they can't be seen. At the last minute, they rush in or jump and grab their victims by the throat. In a good leap, a tiger can cover more than 30 feet.

On some occasions, a tiger turns to eating people. These man-eaters are very dangerous, and many people in India worry that protecting tigers there could make life more dangerous for people.

Scientists have a good idea of what turns a normal man-avoiding tiger into a man-eater. Biologists report that most man-eaters are injured tigers that are unable to hunt their normal prey. These tigers become cattle killers first. Sometimes they attack humans, which are also easy to hunt. Once a tiger has tasted human flesh, it returns for more.

Other attacks on people are probably accidents. Healthy tigers normally avoid people. But if a person comes across a tiger suddenly, the animal may get scared and attack in self-defense.

The problem of man-eating tigers is not as bad as it once was. Indian officials report that about 50 people are killed each year by tigers. Earlier in this century, tigers in India killed more than 800 people each year.

Today, only about 4,000 tigers remain in India, down from 40,000 at the turn of the century. A few hundred more are scattered from Turkey and the Soviet Union to China and parts of Southeast Asia. The giant Siberian tigers are among the most endangered of all cats. Luckily, their numbers seem to be increasing at long last. In the 1930s, fewer than 30 animals survived in the wild. Today, more than 200 roam free.

In recent years, the Indian government has set aside nature preserves for tigers. The animals can live there in safety. Too often, however, villagers move right next to the tigers' preserves to farm and keep their cattle and other animals. In turn, the tigers leave their preserves to capture the farm animals. The villagers fight the tigers, the tigers attack the people, and soon dangerous man-eaters are created.

Tiger hunters in India carry home a tiger that was slain because it ate people. Tigers that attack people are usually too old or crippled to hunt their normal prey.

Scientists agree that people must be protected and their needs must be met if tigers are to be saved from extinction. If villagers can no longer gather firewood in forests where tigers live, other sources of fuel must be supplied. If farmers cannot clear forests to plant crops, other ways to get food must be found. Otherwise, people will have no choice but to enter and clear the forests to get food and firewood. Soon there would be no tigers or wilderness areas left to protect.

In Nepal, a country just north of India, great efforts are being made to make life better for tigers and people. Government workers regularly meet with villagers, school teachers, and community leaders. Then they discuss the problems people are having.

One of the biggest problems these meetings solved was how to help people repair their homes. For years, the people had gathered elephant grass for their roofs from a nearby forest. Then the forest was closed to them and turned into a national park where tigers and other animals could live. This helped the animals, but soon the people needed more grass to patch their roofs. The government saw that the people had a real need, so the park was opened to them one day a year. The park was saved, the tigers were protected, and the people were able to repair their roofs.

ENDANGERED LARGE CATS

1. SNOW LEOPARD
2. JAGUAR

Many other large cats are endangered for the same reasons tigers are in trouble. Some of these cats are considered pests and are killed because they attack people's livestock. All are running out of places to live because their homes are being cleared to make room for people's farms and towns. And even though the law forbids it, all the animals shown here are still killed for their fur.

3. CHEETAH

4. CLOUDED LEOPARD

SMALL CATS

Although the ocelot (above) and the margay (right) are endangered, both animals are illegally hunted in parts of Latin America for their fur. Ocelots once roamed as far as Louisiana and Arkansas, but overhunting years ago eliminated them from most of this country.

The smaller cats are, scientists say, the less we know about them. That may not be true of house cats, but it is true of their small relatives in the wild.

People have spent years studying tigers, lions, and other large cats. We know a lot about how those animals behave, why some are endangered, and what can be done to help them. Even though at least a third of the 30 known species of small cats are also endangered, we don't know nearly as much about them. Small cats are often harder to find. And when scientists apply for financial grants to pay for their research, they find that more money is available for studying large cats than for studying small ones.

At least one endangered small cat—the ocelot—lives in the southwestern United States. This cat, famous for its striped and spotted fur, weighs up to 33 pounds. Ocelots also live farther south, in the forests of Central and South America.

Poaching and habitat loss are the ocelot's main threats. In 1980, a coat made of ocelot fur was worth about $40,000. Killing ocelots is illegal in most countries, but poachers still capture them. Clearing the animal's forest home to make room for farms and ranches is an even bigger problem. Fortunately, some ocelots find safety in parks and refuges.

Margays are another endangered small cat found in North and South America. A single margay was found in Texas more than 100 years ago. It probably had strayed from its normal range in northern Mexico.

Margays are the acrobats of the cat world. Most cats back down a tree hind feet first. Margays go down the other way around, head first. One person wrote that a margay can "drop from branch to branch or dangle from its hind feet like a trapeze artist." The margay's broad, soft feet help it hold on as it climbs and jumps in the treetops.

Margays look a lot like ocelots, but their fur is worth a lot less. Some poachers trim the tails on margay skins so fur buyers will think they're getting ocelot fur. Even though both cats are endangered, traders still illegally sell thousands of their skins around the world.

Andean cats, often called mountain cats, live in the Andes Mountains of Chile, Peru, Bolivia, and Argentina. They were first described in 1865. But more than 100 years passed before scientists were able to study one in the wild. It took scientists 12 years of searching to find just one. After all that time, they were able to watch and photograph the cat for only two hours before it wandered away. It appeared to be about twice the size of a house cat, with striped, silvery fur that helped it hide among the rocks.

Scientists don't know much about the little spotted cat either, even though this cat has been hunted for its fur for many years. It is barely half the size of a house cat. It ap-

parently stays in the thick forests of Central and South America. But as those forests are cleared, the animals are running out of places to find food and raise their young.

Most Spanish lynxes, as the name suggests, live in Spain. They are three to four times as heavy as house cats, and they look like the lynxes that live in Canada and the United States. Some people say that both these lynxes are the same species.

Very little is going well for the Spanish lynx these days. A virus killed many of the rabbits that the cat eats. Forests where the lynx lives are being cleared for farmland. New roads bring more traffic through lynx habitat, and the animals are no match for cars that hit them.

Africa's black-footed cats are the world's smallest cats. One of them weighs only about four pounds, less than a small bag of sugar or flour. These cats hunt by night, eating everything from lizards and birds to beetles and shrews. They sleep during the day, usually in old termite mounds or the burrows left behind by other animals.

People disagree over how many black-footed cats are left. One report says they are endangered, and another says they aren't. Identifying these cats in the wild is not easy. They look a lot like African wild cats, so some people who report sighting those animals may really be seeing black-footed cats.

No one disputes the fact that Asia's small cats are endangered. One of them, the Iriomote cat, is among the rarest cats in the world. Only a few dozen are left, living on a small Japanese island east of Taiwan.

Scientists first discovered this cat in the 1960s, although local people had known about it for years. Despite being protected by Japanese law, the Iriomote cat is dying out. People are clearing the jungle where it lives and killing the wild pigs it normally hunts.

Loss of habitat is one of the main reasons the rest of Asia's small cats are in trouble. These cats are not hunted for their fur, though some end up on family dinner tables.

The flat-headed cat is one of the strangest cats in Asia. It looks like it ran headfirst into

Many Spanish lynxes (left) died from lack of food when the rabbits they hunt started to die out. Asia's Iriomote cat (below) has a problem finding enough wild pigs to eat.

a closed door. Its long, sloping face and strong jaw muscles are just right, though, for catching fish, one of its favorite foods.

The Asian golden cat is better known as the "fire tiger" in Burma and Thailand. Some people there believe that carrying one of the cat's hairs protects them from tigers. Like many other small cats, the Asian golden cat is shy and hard to find. It has been seen in many countries, from India and Nepal to southern China and some nearby islands.

Scientists don't know very much about the marbled cat, either. It looks like a leopard the size of a large house cat. It lives in the forests of South Asia, where it preys on birds and squirrels in the trees.

Only two continents have no endangered small cats. How did Australia and Antarctica avoid this problem? Simple. They have no native cats at all.

CROCODILES

Farming and fashion are among a crocodile's worst enemies. From the smallest crocodile to the largest, almost all these animals are endangered. In some places, their swampy homes have been drained to make room for people's farms and towns. Some of the animals, and their eggs, have been taken for food. A few have been killed for sport or for revenge whenever they attack people or pets or livestock. But most crocodiles are killed for their skin. Crocodile hides make fashionable—and expensive—leather.

When you mention crocodiles to some people, the first thing they think is "Man eater!" Extra-large mouths and sharp teeth make all 11 kinds of crocodiles look fierce. But only two kinds—salt-water and Nile crocodiles—attack people very often.

After the baby Nile crocodile at left breaks out of its shell, it faces danger from hungry mongooses, baboons, and other enemies. The mother crocodile sometimes protects her youngster by carrying it in her mouth (above).

The salt-water crocodile—often called a "saltie"—is perhaps the most dangerous. It is also one of the largest and most widespread of all crocodiles. One writer called the saltie "21 feet of bad temper encased in armor." A crocodile that long weighs more than a ton. Salties can be found from eastern India to the Philippines and northern Australia.

Hunters in Australia tell of salties biting chunks out of their boats' propellers and leaving deep tooth marks in the sides of the boats. A crocodile can close its jaws with enough strength to break the bones of a cow.

Like all crocodiles, salties use their teeth for grabbing, not chewing. Small salties feed mostly on insects, snails, and small fish. Larger salties capture larger prey, from turtles and snakes to rats and geese. Some adult salties have been known to feed on sharks.

If a saltie or other crocodile catches prey too large to swallow, it simply twists around and around until it tears its victim into smaller pieces. Although a saltie can eat an entire horse in two days, it can also wait a long time between meals. Some go six months to a year without eating at all.

When scientists catch a saltie or other crocodile alive, they first tie the animal's jaws shut. The rope doesn't have to be too strong. The muscles that pull the jaws open are weak. A grown man has no problem holding a large crocodile's or alligator's jaws shut with his hands. Performers who wrestle alligators know this. They just have to be careful when they finally let go.

The other end of the animal is dangerous, too. Some crocodiles attack by swinging their strong tails and knocking down their prey. A large crocodile can break a canoe in half with one blow of its tail.

Africa's Nile crocodiles are also man-eaters—sometimes. Normally, they feed on fish. In some parts of Africa, people are glad to have these crocodiles around. They eat the kinds of fish that people don't want. With less competition for food, the fish that the people like grow bigger and bigger.

Like the rest of their relatives, baby Nile crocodiles have faces that only a mother could love. And mother Nile crocodiles really do take care of their young. After burying her eggs in a sand bank, the female settles down nearby and waits. No hungry baboon or mongoose or other animal can eat these eggs while she stands guard.

After more than two months, the eggs start to hatch. The mother scrapes away the sand so the youngsters can get out. When the mother puts these youngsters into her mouth, she's not eating them. She's carrying them safely so enemies can't get at them.

The smallest of all crocodiles is not dangerous, but it is endangered. It is the Congo dwarf crocodile of central Africa, and it is about the length of a yardstick. Other than its size, scientists don't know very much about this rare creature. It lives in freshwater streams that flow into the Zaire River. When scientists discovered this crocodile, early in the 20th century, the Zaire was called the Congo. That's how the creature got its name.

The American crocodile is one of the world's largest. Some measure more than 20 feet long. Most are found in swamps, bays, and rivers from Mexico southward to Peru. Not many people have seen this rare creature in the wild in the United States. Here it is found only in southern Florida, south of Miami. Its smaller relative, the American alligator, is much more common.

Is there hope for saving these creatures? Yes, if the laws protecting the animals are obeyed. Buying or selling endangered crocodiles' skins is illegal in many places. Help for many crocodiles may also come from the animal farms of Africa, Australia, and other countries. Crocodiles are raised there to be harvested for their valuable skins. That takes the pressure off the animals in the wild. In addition, some of the farms raise so many crocodiles that the extra ones are released to begin new lives in the wild.

Not all crocodile skins are taken illegally. The New Guinea villager at left shows off a skin from an animal accidentally caught in a fishing net. The animals sunbathing at right live on an African crocodile farm, where they are raised to be harvested. By using only farm-raised animals, people can leave endangered wild crocodiles alone.

GORILLA

orillas in danger? That's hard to believe! These animals look too big and powerful for anyone to bother. Even leopards normally leave gorillas alone. Leopards look for prey that is easy to catch. They don't want to fight a creature that is almost six feet tall and weighs more than 400 pounds. Unless they are protecting themselves, though, gorillas are normally very gentle. They eat only plants and often sneak away when people come near.

Gorillas live in Africa in the jungle lowlands along the equator and in jungles in the mountains. Scientists haven't studied the lowland gorillas so they aren't sure how

many live there. Estimates range from 5,000 to 15,000. But scientists have studied mountain gorillas. These gorillas live on the slopes of dead volcanoes that spread into three countries: Zaire, Uganda, and Rwanda.

Once, at least 500 gorillas lived around these volcanoes. In recent years, the number has dropped to less than half that. The gorillas' worst enemy is man. Killing gorillas is against the law now, but at one time people killed the animals and sold their heads and hands as souvenirs. In some places, people may still hunt gorillas and use parts of their bodies in voodoo rituals.

One of the worst problems for mountain gorillas is finding enough room to gather food and raise families. A lot of people with nowhere else to go are moving into the areas where the gorillas live. The people clear the land to make room for homes and farms.

When gorillas are left alone, they live simple lives. They stay in groups of up to 20 or so animals. An adult male leads each group. Adult males are called silverbacks. If you look at the picture on page 49 you can see why. A silverback's back is covered with silvery hair. An average troop includes the leader, a slightly younger male, three or four females, and up to half a dozen youngsters.

Gorilla groups are a lot like human families in many ways. The baby gorillas weigh just a bit less than human babies. The older

When a gorilla mother first nurses her baby (right), the youngster is so weak it can barely hold on. After about six months, it easily climbs trees by itself (left).

46

youngsters like to play. They swing on vines, toss and tumble on the ground, and play follow-the-leader. And, when they don't get their own way, they have temper tantrums.

Gorillas often yawn and stretch when waking up in the morning. When one catches a bad cold, its eyes water and its nose runs. Gorillas in captivity also catch pneumonia easily and sometimes die from it.

Gorillas spend most of their lives eating and sleeping. The group follows its leader, the silverback, as he moves through the thick jungle gathering leaves, fruit, flowers, and roots. These animals are definitely *not* dainty eaters. A hungry gorilla stuffs leaves into its mouth with one hand while grabbing more food with the other.

Are the best leaves near the top of a tall tree? No problem. Even the heaviest gorillas find climbing easy.

After a day of napping and gnawing, the group settles down for the night. Some gorillas climb trees and fold down branches to make beds. Others fold over bushes on the ground. This all takes less than five minutes. Gorillas have no permanent place they call home. They're happy sleeping wherever they happen to be when the sun goes down. They rarely use the same nest twice.

As long as no one bothers them, gorillas are peaceful and gentle. But if they think they're in danger, watch out! That's when they attack. You don't want to get in the way of an angry gorilla.

A gorilla will give you plenty of warning that it's going to attack. It calls out—first softly and slowly, then louder and faster. Then it rips off branches and brush and throws them into the air. Now comes the part you've probably seen in the movies. The gorilla slaps its hands against its chest. It may even slap a tree trunk.

If all this doesn't scare you away, the gorilla has one last trick. It runs right at you, then stops short and WHAM! pounds the ground with its hand.

Will a gorilla really hit you? It might, especially if you run. Then it might also chase you and give you a nasty bite.

As long as you don't scare or threaten them, gorillas will leave you alone. After a while, they will ignore you and go on about their business. This fact has helped make gorilla-watching a tourist attraction in Africa. And it may help save the animals' lives.

When visitors pay to see gorillas in the wild, people living in the area earn money to support themselves and their families. They don't need to cut down the jungle to raise food or capture gorillas to sell. The people are helped. The land is preserved. And an endangered animal is saved from extinction.

Light hairs on the back of adult male gorillas give them the nickname "silverback." The 500-pound silverback above will attack if threatened, but it easily adjusts to the presence of humans. Guides now help tourists watch gorillas without disturbing them (left).

PEREGRINE FALCON

They can fly as fast as a small airplane. Kings have kept them as pets. Over the past 50 years, a poisonous pesticide nearly wiped them out. Some of them now live on the roofs of skyscrapers.

What bird fits this weird description? A peregrine falcon.

Peregrine falcons live all over the world, and three kinds live in North America. Peregrines belong to a group of birds known as raptors, or birds of prey. Raptors hunt and kill other animals for food.

Peregrines normally eat doves, ducks, and other birds, which they catch in midair. A hungry falcon will circle high in the sky, soaring above the height at which most birds fly. Its cruising speed is 40 to 60 miles per hour. When it spots a likely meal, it dives straight at it. During this dive, known as the stoop, the falcon slices through the air at close to 200 miles per hour. A diving peregrine is the fastest bird in the world.

The falcon strikes with its feet so its sharp, curved claws—called talons—can hold onto its victim. Sometimes the other bird flies out of reach at the last minute. But if the attacking falcon hits its target, the smaller bird usually dies instantly.

There is another side to the life of this superb hunter. It provides for and protects its family. Most peregrines nest along the ledges of steep cliffs. The nesting spot is called an *eyrie* (rhymes with merry).

Peregrines mate for life, and they return each year to the same eyrie. In North America, the peregrine males return from the south in late February or March. First, a male reclaims his cliff and eyrie. The eyrie often overlooks a wide area, and the bird can spot both enemies and prey from the nest.

The female arrives about three weeks later. Larger than her mate, she is able to strike down larger prey. When the pair hunts together, she makes the first attack. If she misses, her mate may try to make the kill.

Soon the female falcon lays her eggs. The chicks hatch around April or May. Both peregrine parents take good care of the chicks, bringing them food and guarding the eyrie. Until they learn to fly, the chicks' greatest danger is falling from the ledge. As they hop about, a gust of wind could send them tumbling to the bottom of the cliff.

After five or six weeks, the young peregrines begin to fly. They learn to hunt by

Peregrine chicks keep their parents busy. One parent guards the nest (left) while the other cruises the skies (above), searching for small birds to feed the family. A peregrine usually flies at the speed of a car on the highway, but when it dives to attack prey, it reaches nearly 200 miles per hour.

following and imitating their parents. In a few months, they can catch their own food. By the time peregrines migrate in the fall, the youngsters are ready to take off on their own.

This swift hunter has fascinated humans throughout the ages. Falconry, the ancient sport of hunting with trained falcons, probably began in China or Persia over four thousand years ago. Kings and noblemen hired falconers, experts who helped them train and care for the birds. Falconers used several kinds of birds of prey for hunting, but they favored peregrines. Like other falcons, peregrines could be trained to hunt at people's commands. But only peregrines could be readily trained to circle the skies, waiting for the human hunters on the ground to flush prey into the open. Then the falcon would swoop down for the kill.

When scientists raise peregrines in captivity, they use falcon-shaped puppets to feed the baby birds. The youngsters learn to expect food from other falcons, not people. At the same time, the scientists can study the birds up close without scaring them.

Although people prize these birds, people's activities almost wiped them out. In the 1960s, scientists checking on peregrine nesting sites in the eastern United States found that every one had been abandoned. The birds in that area were extinct. The problem was not just a local one. Fewer and fewer peregrines were found in the rest of the country and in Canada and Europe as well.

At first, no one could understand why the birds were disappearing. But scientists soon discovered the answer: DDT, a powerful poison once used to kill insects on crops.

The falcons didn't eat crops or the poisoned insects, so how did crop spray end up poisoning the peregrines? The problem lay in other birds that did eat the dead insects. DDT in the insects entered these birds' bodies and stayed there. Then peregrines fed on the insect-eating birds. More and more DDT built up inside the falcons. It didn't kill them, but it caused their chicks to die.

DDT destroyed the ability of female peregrines to lay strong eggs. The shells of eggs laid by the poisoned birds were too thin. They could not hold the weight of the adult sitting on them to keep them warm. When the eggs collapsed, the unhatched chicks died. Peregrines were doomed until countries started controlling the use of DDT. Now, there is hope for their recovery.

The goal now is to restore the bird to the eastern United States and increase its populations in the other states and in Canada. To do this, scientists in both countries are raising baby peregrines in captivity. Getting these peregrines ready for life in the wild is difficult. Scientists try to treat the chicks the way their real parents would. They even use a puppet shaped like a peregrine to feed the chicks. The idea is to help the chicks learn to recognize and identify with their own kind.

Researchers usually place these hand-raised birds where peregrines once lived, but they also release a few atop city skyscrapers. Cities make good homes for falcons. The tall buildings provide all the advantages of a cliff —protection from enemies and a view of an area where they can search for prey. What

52

can peregrines find to eat in a city? Maybe you've already guessed—pigeons.

Today, peregrines are making a comeback. Scientists in Canada and the United States all report success in releasing peregrines that were born in captivity. Colorado alone released more than 300 birds in the 1970s and '80s. It may sound strange, but the goal of these programs is to go out of business. That can only happen when the peregrines are making it on their own.

Most peregrines raised in captivity are later released in wild places, but some of the birds are let loose in cities. Peregrines like to perch high up on cliffs (right) and on skyscrapers (below), where they can spot their prey from a long way away.

NUMBAT, WOMBAT, AND WALLABY

Australia is almost as large as the United States, but it has fewer people than New York State. You might think that with so much space and so few people Australia would not have any endangered animals. But it does. Australian animals are unique, but they face the same problems that are threatening endangered animals all over the world.

Part of the problem is Australia's climate. Most of the land is hot, dry desert. Places that have water are in big demand by people and animals. When forests are logged and brushland cleared for farms and towns, the animals can't find the food and shelter they need to survive.

Australian animals also face other problems besides loss of habitat. When Europeans came to Australia, they wanted to hunt the animals they had hunted at home. Australia had no rabbits or foxes, so the Europeans brought some with them. They also brought goats for milk and meat.

These animals had no enemies in their new home. The rabbits and goats quickly multiplied. They soon overran the countryside, taking over land needed by farmers and native wildlife. And the foxes easily killed many of the native animals, which had not evolved any defenses against this predator they had never faced before.

Today, the most endangered Australian animals are some of the odd-looking little creatures known as wallabies, wombats, and numbats. These animals belong to a group called marsupials. The word *marsupial* comes from a Latin word meaning "pouch." Almost all marsupial mothers have pouches on their abdomens. When marsupial babies are born, they crawl into their mother's pouch. There they find nipples, from which they suck milk. For the next few months, the tiny babies don't budge. They just drink milk until they grow big and strong enough to begin life in the outside world.

Wallabies come in many sizes and have pouches just like their bigger relatives, the kangaroos. Some wallabies are only a foot tall when fully grown. Others grow up to three feet tall and weigh about 50 pounds. They have beautiful fur, ranging from brown to rust to gray. Some, such as the rock

Australia's hairy-nosed wombats (above) and yellow-footed rock wallabies (left) nearly died out because of overhunting and loss of habitat. Today, these animals find safe places to live in refuges.

wallabies, have rings around their tails and stripes on their faces and backs. Yellow-footed rock wallabies were once hunted for their fur until they almost became extinct.

All wallabies have strong tails that are nearly as long as the animal is tall. The tail acts like a third leg. The wallaby leans on it when resting and uses it for balance as it hops across the grasslands and rocks.

Rock wallabies also have feet that are specially adapted to their habitat. The rough, well-padded soles of their feet give them a good grip on rocks and boulders. With their strong back legs, yellow-footed rock wallabies can leap distances of up to 13 feet in one jump. That's about the length of a small car.

Wombats, on the other hand, don't do any leaping at all. These furry, bulldog-sized creatures can gallop almost as fast as a horse for short distances. But wombats mainly use their powerful front legs, along with their sharp, beaverlike teeth, to dig underground burrows.

A wombat is almost impossible to pull out of its burrow if it doesn't want to come. The stocky beast stuffs itself headfirst into a tunnel. When anything tries to get a grip on its tough hide, the wombat smashes against the tunnel wall. A human hand or dog's nose caught between the wombat and the wall may get broken.

The wombat's pouch is also specially adapted for tunneling. Wombat pouches

The numbat uses its long tongue to pull termites from trees and logs in its forest home (above and left). The koala (top left) is one Australian animal that has made a comeback. It is no longer in danger of becoming extinct.

open *backwards*. While mom digs, the youngster safely looks out between her back legs. That's a lot better than getting a face full of dirt!

Although it is also a marsupial, the numbat doesn't have a pouch. Instead, female numbats have long hair and folds of skin on their stomachs around their nipples. This extra skin and hair protect the numbat's growing babies.

Numbat babies have to hang on tightly. Their mother does a lot of running around to find termites to eat—up to 20,000 a day! Numbats use their skinny tongues to pull termites out of their tunnels in the soil. A numbat's tongue is half as long as its body.

Some people call the numbat the prettiest animal in Australia. Its rust-colored coat is accented by several white stripes across its back. And it often carries its fuzzy tail up over its back like a banner.

Many Australians realize that their native animals are unique national treasures. Scientists there are tracking wallabies and numbats to learn how they live and what they need to survive. Other people are working to reduce the bad effects of foxes and rabbits and other animals that are not native to Australia. Bit by bit the people are fencing off areas where all non-native plants and animals have been removed. This protects the native species so they can grow and thrive. The government is also helping by setting aside larger areas for refuges, much like the national parks in the United States.

Will these efforts save the endangered animals? Australians think so. They already have one success story behind them: the koala. For years, koalas were hunted for their valuable fur. In addition, their forest homes were being cut down. At one point, koalas had completely disappeared from some parts of the country. Finally, killing koalas was outlawed. Scientists also raised the animals in captivity and returned them to the wild. Today, koalas have returned to many areas where they formerly lived. Australians now hope to repeat this success with the endangered wallabies, wombats, and numbats.

NENE GOOSE

Hundreds of thousands of years ago, some migrating geese got lost. No one will ever know how they got lost. Maybe a storm separated the geese from the rest of their flock.

The lost geese landed on one or more islands in Hawaii. Although the volcanic island was different from their normal home, the geese survived. Soon, they laid eggs and young geese hatched. These youngsters grew up and had goslings of their own. Over the years, each new generation of geese changed a little bit. Eventually, the geese grew so different from their ancestors that they became a new species: the nene goose.

For thousands of years, the nene geese survived quite well in Hawaii. In fact, the Hawaiian Islands were once a perfect place for many birds to live. Since no bird-eating animals lived on the islands, the birds had no enemies. Nearly 100 other species of birds found nowhere else made their homes in Hawaii. The first Hawaiians ate nene geese and decorated clothing with feathers from the islands' colorful birds. But in those early times, even humans didn't threaten Hawaii's birds very much.

As more and more people came to the islands, they brought only trouble for the birds. People shot birds in greater numbers.

Whalers stopped by the islands to stock up on salted goose to eat during their long sea journeys. Worst of all, people brought goats, cattle, horses, and sheep to the islands. These animals destroyed the birds' nests and ate the plants that the birds needed.

Rats also came to Hawaii on the ships. To keep the rats from destroying crops, people brought mongooses to the island. This was a big mistake. Mongooses do eat rats —when they can find them. But mongooses hunt during the day and rats come out mostly at night. So when hungry mongooses were on the prowl, all they could find to eat were birds and bird eggs. This was bad news for all the Hawaiian birds. In 1800, about 25,000 nene geese thrived in Hawaii. By 1952, only about 30 remained.

The story of the nene goose almost ended in the 1950s. But Sir Peter Scott, a British wildlife painter, came to the rescue. He headed an organization that helped wild birds. He took a pair of the geese to a protected park in Slimbridge, England. There, he hoped to breed them and start new flocks. Over the past 40 years, more than 2,000 geese have been raised at Slimbridge. More than 200 of them have been sent back to Hawaii. In the meantime, Hawaiians have

Although they look a little like Canada geese, which are common in North America, Hawaii's nene geese are among the rarest birds in the world. Other geese like water and migrate long distances in spring and fall, but not nene geese. They stay put all year near their homes on dry lava beds.

also helped by creating protected areas where the geese can live in safety.

Today, the nene goose is Hawaii's state bird. More than 500 of them live on the islands of Hawaii and Maui. These geese may look rather ordinary, but they have had quite an extraordinary history.

ENDANGERED HAWAIIAN BIRDS

The nene goose seems to be making a comeback, but Hawaii has more endangered bird species than any other state in the U.S. At least 23 Hawaiian birds have become extinct in the last 100 years. More than 30 are endangered. The colorful birds shown here represent only a few of these.

1. CRESTED HONEYCREEPER
2. MAUI PARROTBILL
3. HAWAIIAN THRUSH
4. HAWAII 'AKEPA
5. MAUI 'AKEPA
6. 'AKIALOA

LEMURS

For lemurs, long-tailed animals that look a bit like monkeys, Madagascar was once a Garden of Eden. Madagascar is an island the size of Texas. It is 1,000 miles long and lies off the coast of southeastern Africa. At one time, about forty kinds of lemurs lived there. One kind grew as large as a St. Bernard dog. The lemurs had few enemies and lots of food and shelter. They also had fascinating neighbors: giant tortoises, pygmy hippos, and 500-pound birds that laid eggs the size of soccer balls.

Then, about 1,500 years ago, people moved to Madagascar. These settlers started clearing the forests for farmland. They also killed lemurs to eat. After a while, many lemurs had no place to live. Some scientists think that changes in the weather or other causes may have added to the lemurs' problems. Whatever the reasons, many lemurs were doomed. At least a dozen kinds, including all the giant ones, became extinct. The lemurs that are left are all endangered.

Mouse lemurs are the smallest kinds of all. Some weigh less than a candy bar. A dozen of them sitting on a scale would weigh only a pound. These creatures are so hard to find that one species of mouse lemur was not identified until 1986.

All lemurs are noisy. When forked lemurs get together, their voices sound like loud static on a radio. They make noises for many reasons. The youngsters call when they are separated from their mothers. The adults greet each other when they meet. And they all raise an alarm when they see danger.

The creatures known as sportive lemurs are the homebodies of the lemur world. Their lives are simple: they get by with very little effort. During the day, they sleep in holes in trees. Even when they are awake at night, they spend a lot of time sitting and staring. Their large eyes help them see when there is little light.

Sportive lemurs live in a dry part of Madagascar where food is hard to find. When they spot a rich supply of leaves or flowers, they make a few leaps and settle down to eat. After that, they sit quietly until they become hungry again.

Ring-tailed lemurs (left) prefer to travel on the ground. When they do take to the trees, they use large, horizontal limbs as walkways. The fat-tailed dwarf lemur (above) hibernates in its den during the winter. That's the dry season in some parts of Madagascar, when food is scarce and hard to find.

Most kinds of lemurs have no problem climbing and jumping from limb to limb. Even if a branch breaks, a leaping lemur can usually grab another branch. But every now and then a lemur misses and falls all the way to the ground. One scientist watched a lemur fall almost 50 feet, bounce, then run back up the nearest tree.

Just over half of the lemur species do their running, jumping, and eating at night. Most of the others spend the night sleeping. They eat, mate, and raise their young during the day. Brown lemurs, however, don't seem to mind whether it's daylight or dark. They eat and sleep around the clock.

Brown lemurs also do something scientists once thought few animals ever do: they sometimes share their food. It's interesting to watch one of them split a fruit into two pieces and give half to another lemur.

Ring-tailed lemurs aren't quite so considerate, at least when the males show off. When a male ring-tail wants to show that he's the boss, he challenges another male to a stink-fight. The stink comes from oil given off by glands on his arms and chest.

Two males in a stink-fight stand facing each other. They rub their tails with their hands, smearing on the smelly oil. For up to an hour, the two males face off, waving their stinking tails at each other. If one of the lemurs edges forward, the other one backs up. Finally, one of them gives up, makes a squeaky noise, and runs away.

If a male starts a stink-fight with a female, he may be in for a surprise. Instead of running away, a female lemur is more likely to turn and punch the male in the head.

Lemurs normally seem content to feed peacefully on insects, leaves, flowers, and fruit. At least one lemur, Verreaux's (vair-OHS) sifaka, gets all the water it needs from its food. Other lemurs drink from streams and even lick the wet leaves after a rain.

During the dry season, fat-tailed dwarf lemurs give up trying to find food or water. They spend up to eight months hibernating deep in hollow tree trunks. They survive the season living on the fat stored in their tails.

Saving lemurs will not be easy because Madagascar's problems are so hard to solve. People there are poor, they need food, they need homes, and they need firewood. Clearing the forests for firewood and timber or to make room for farms helps people survive. But it leaves lemurs no place to live.

Fortunately, the people of Madagascar love their lemurs. They don't want the animals to disappear. So far, they have set aside nearly a dozen areas where all animals and plants are protected. The next step is to meet the people's needs so these areas can be maintained.

The mouse lemur (left) is so small that several young ones could fit into a teacup. The white-fronted lemur (above) is one of 13 lemur species being studied at a North Carolina research center.

1. AYE-AYE

2. ANGULATED TORTOISE

3. INDRI

4. SIFAKA

5. AVAHI

6. RADIATED TORTOISE

Although the island of Madagascar is as large as Texas, animals there are running out of places to live. Land is cleared for crops, and forests are cut down for fuel and timber. All the creatures shown here are endangered, and at least 17 other kinds have died out since the first people arrived on the island 1,500 years ago.

ENDANGERED
ANIMALS OF MADAGASCAR

BLACK RHINO

People are at war over rhinos. This isn't a war between enemy countries. It is a war between people who try to save rhinos and people who want to kill them.

The animal's full name is rhinoceros, which means "nose-horned." Most people say rhino for short. Africa has two kinds of rhino; Asia has three. All are endangered.

Most of the trouble for rhinos comes from poachers, people who kill the animals illegally. Lions and hyenas sometimes eat baby rhinos, but grown-up rhinos are too large for most animals to bother. In fact, rhinos are the world's second-largest land animals. Only elephants are larger.

Some of the worst poaching is going on in Africa, where most of the world's rhinos live. Poachers don't kill for fun or to be mean. These people are poor, and one rhino horn can bring them as much money as they could normally earn in a year. They sell some rhino horns to be ground up and put into medicine. And at least one Middle Eastern country smuggles in rhino horns to make the handles of expensive daggers.

People in many Asian countries use rhino-horn medicine to treat fever, arthritis, bad eyesight, and other health problems. Does this medicine really work? Scientists haven't found that it does. But as long as people believe in it, they will continue to pay huge sums of money to get it. In 1985, some rhino horns brought more than $13,000 a pound. Poachers got only a little of that money, but it was enough to make them want to kill more rhinos.

Poachers in Africa most often go after black rhinos. These creatures are easier to find, and often less protected, than the white rhinos. At one time, black rhinos were one of the most widespread rhinos of all. Hundreds of thousands of these animals could be found south of the Sahara Desert. Some lived on the grassy plains. Others preferred the thick brush at the edge of forests. To eat, they used their strong lips to strip the leaves from bushes and shrubs. As long as they had food and water, they were content. Many African animals still follow the tracks to water that black rhinos cleared through the bush. By the mid-1980s, fewer than 5,000 black rhinos survived.

Africa's black rhino (left) weighs up to 3,000 pounds and runs faster than a man. Poachers kill black rhinos for their valuable horns (above).

69

A black rhino is not black at all. It is dark gray and is called "black" to distinguish it from its close relative, the white rhino. A white rhino isn't white, either. Its name started out as "weit" (WITE) rhino, a name that means "wide" rhino. The "wide" refers to the animal's extra-wide mouth.

A black rhino is dangerous if it knows someone is getting close. It can't see well, but it has good senses of smell and hearing. If it smells or hears someone, it often charges. Despite its size, it moves quickly. Getting hit by a 3,000-pound rhino going 25 miles an hour is like getting hit by a car.

Some unlucky victims have been tossed into the air by one of the black rhino's two large horns. The front horn normally measures between two and four feet long. A rhino's horns are solid, but they are not made of bone. Instead, they are made of thin fibers a lot like human hair, all stuck together.

Like all rhinos, a black rhino cannot sweat. Instead, it soaks in water or mud to keep cool. Mud also keeps the rhino's skin flexible and protects it from parasites. When the mud dries and falls off, it pulls off ticks and lice that were stuck to the skin.

Birds also help keep a rhino clean. In Africa, oxpeckers hop all over both black and white rhinos and pick off insects. The birds get an easy meal, but they do more than keep the rhinos free of pests. They also fly off with loud cries when they see people. That helps alert the rhinos when poachers come near.

Some black rhinos set up territories, areas where they find food and raise their young. A territory may be a mile across or barely the size of a football field. If the food or water runs out, those rhinos are in trouble, for they will not leave their territories. In the 1960s, several hundred black rhinos died in a drought. They could have found water and food if they had moved a few miles away.

Drought and poachers aren't the black rhino's only enemies. In one country, more than 1,000 black rhinos were killed to make some land safe for farming.

Is there hope for the black rhino and the rest of the world's rhinos? Yes, but a lot must be done. People need a substitute for rhino products. Medicine shops in Burma already sell "artificial dried rhino blood" in place of real rhino blood for medicine. In Japan, some people substitute dried worms for rhino horns to treat fever.

At the same time, the few rhinos that are left can be protected in parks and nature preserves. Some African and Asian countries have already begun moving the animals to safety. Poachers don't want to quit, though, so rangers in Kenya and Zimbabwe are told to shoot poachers on sight.

Protection does work, though it will take time for the number of rhinos to increase enough for the animals to be out of danger. Africa's white rhinos are already on the road to recovery. At the beginning of the 20th century, people thought these giant creatures were extinct. Then a small group was found in South Africa. Land was set aside where these animals could live in peace. They

This five-week-old rhino calf will stay with its mother (left) until just after the next year's calf is born. The red-billed birds sitting on the rhinos are oxpeckers, which eat insects and other parasites they find. A healthy adult rhino has nothing to fear from a nearby pride of lions (above). Humans are the worst enemies rhinos face.

multiplied quickly, and soon white rhinos were being sent to other countries.

White rhinos are still endangered, but they have been saved from near-certain extinction. Saving the white rhino is a conservation success story. The next step is to do the same for the black rhino and all the other endangered rhinos.

1. JAVAN RHINO

2. GREAT INDIAN RHINO

ENDANGERED RHINOS

Too large to be threatened by other animals, rhinos have only one serious enemy: humans. By taking over the animals' lands for farming or killing them for their horns, people have almost killed off every species of rhino. Some scientists worry that if current efforts to protect the animals fail, no rhinos will be left by the year 2000.

3. WHITE RHINO
4. SUMATRAN RHINO

MURIQUI

In the jungles of South America, a Brazilian plantation owner is working hard to save an endangered monkey. The man is Feliciano Miguel Abdala. The monkey is the muriqui (moo-ree-KEE), also known as the woolly spider monkey.

What can one man do to save an endangered species of monkey? Actually, it is what he is *not* doing that helps. Mr. Abdala owns a coffee plantation called Montes Claros, which includes four square miles of jungle. He won't let anyone burn this jungle or cut it down. He won't allow anyone to kill the monkeys there or trap them to sell.

These efforts protect the animals as well as their homes and food supplies. Muriquis are one of the world's rarest animals. About 300 are left, and they all live in the jungles of South America. They are South America's largest monkey and the largest mammal in Brazil. They weigh up to 30 pounds and measure about five feet long—including their tail. About 50 of the monkeys live at Montes Claros. For now, those few are safe.

Two groups of muriquis live on Mr. Abdala's plantation. By studying these monkey families, called troops, scientists have learned a lot about how muriquis live.

Muriquis never leave the forest. In fact, they hardly ever leave the trees. They spend most of their days swinging through the thick jungle, searching for fruits and leaves to eat. Fruit is more nutritious, and the monkeys prefer it to leaves. Muriquis travel up to two miles a day through dense jungle. When they do eat leaves, the monkeys must pack a lot into their stomachs to get full.

A muriqui troop leads a peaceful life compared with some other monkey groups. Muriquis hardly ever fight. In many monkey species, the males fight each other to decide which one gets to mate with a female. But muriquis rarely hurt each other and often share the same mate. In many species, the bigger and stronger males bully the females. But muriqui males and females grow to be about equal size and strength, and they get along quite well. Because they live so far up in the trees, it's a good thing muriquis don't push each other around too much. A fall from a high branch could kill one of them. Scientists think the threat of falling could be one reason why the muriquis don't fight.

Muriquis climb safely through the trees by using their feet and their tails as well as their hands. How? A muriqui's feet can make a

Brazil's largest mammal, the 30-pound muriqui spends its entire life in the trees. Barely 300 survive today.

fist and grab onto branches just as its hands do. Its tail is *prehensile,* which means it can also hold onto things. This tail is lined with a firm pad that gives it a tight grip. The tail is also flexible enough to wrap tightly around small branches. A hungry muriqui can hang by its tail and stuff food into its mouth with both hands. It's as if the monkey had five hands: one on each arm, one on each leg, and one on its tail.

The survival of these monkeys depends on the survival of the jungle where they live. Explorers first landed in Brazil 500 years ago. Then, the Atlantic rain forest stretched along the entire coast of the country. It covered an area as large as Texas and New Mexico combined. Over 400,000 muriquis lived in the jungle then. Today, only about two percent of the original Atlantic rain forest remains. The amount left would barely cover the small state of Maryland. The 300 muriquis that are left live in tiny pockets of forest like the jungle at Montes Claros.

These small areas of jungle are like islands. Instead of being surrounded by ocean, though, they are surrounded by farmland, industrial areas, and cities.

Since a muriqui never leaves its own area, it can't breed with monkeys that live in another area. This could create a problem for a muriqui population that is already dangerously low. If disease wiped out the female muriquis at Montes Claros, for example, the males would not be able to find mates.

The small size of these patches of jungle also limits the amount of food available to the monkeys that live there. Lack of food keeps small troops like those in Montes Claros from increasing their numbers. If too many more monkeys were born in the small jungle island, food would become too scarce to go around. Some monkeys would starve.

What has happened to destroy so much of the forest? The human population of Brazil continues to increase, and people need the land and resources of the jungle. People clear the rain forest to make way for farms, factories, and cities. They cut down the trees to make lumber for wood products. Two of

the world's largest cities, Sao Paulo and Rio de Janeiro, cover over 900 square miles of land that once was jungle.

But people are learning to care about muriquis and about the rain forest. Teachers now travel throughout Brazil, showing pictures of muriquis and describing how the monkeys live. They teach people to let the monkeys roam free and not to kill or capture them. Muriquis also appear on postage stamps, T-shirts, and posters. Today they are a symbol of the endangered rain forest and of all the animals that live there.

The muriqui's strong, prehensile tail acts like an extra hand (left). The monkey uses it for support while moving through the 60-foot-high treetops, and holds on to limbs with it when eating with both hands. The muriqui is a symbol of the conservation movement in Brazil. It appears on postage stamps (left inset) and on posters used to teach villagers the importance of saving their country's wildlife (above).

1. GOLDEN LION TAMARIN
2. GOELDI'S MARMOSET
3. HOWLER MONKEY
4. BARE-FACED TAMARIN
5. RED UAKARI
6. BUFFY TUFTED-EAR MARMOSET

Muriquis are not the only monkeys in trouble. Throughout the world, many monkeys are in danger of becoming extinct. In South America alone, at least 13 monkeys, including those shown on this page, face the same problems as the muriqui. Their jungle homes are being cut and burned, and they themselves are being killed for food or captured and sold as pets.

ENDANGERED BRAZILIAN MONKEYS

GREEN SEA TURTLE

They fed the British Navy as it cruised the shores of the New World. They provided fresh meat for Spanish fleets returning eastward to their home port of Cadiz. *They* are the green sea turtles, some of the most valuable reptiles in the world.

Now endangered in many places, sea turtles and their eggs are protected by law in the United States and many other countries. However, some nations don't have such laws, or don't enforce them. Green sea turtles continue to be used by people. Their skins are turned into leather, and their eggs and meat are eaten by villagers from Turkey to Thailand. Catching green sea turtles and harvesting their eggs is a big business.

Some people capture turtles from boats, catching them in nets or harpooning them when they swim near the surface. Many others wait to catch the nesting females when they come ashore.

Some fishermen in Cuba and a few other places use the strangest fishing tackle of all: remoras (REM-or-ahs), also called suckerfish. These fish have suction pads on their heads. They stick the pads to sharks, turtles, and other large sea creatures and get free rides. Turtle fishermen fasten a line to a remora, then toss the fish into the water. Once the fish latches onto a turtle, the fisherman hauls in the catch.

Even when people leave them alone, it's amazing that green sea turtles survive natural dangers, from raccoons on the beach to

Baby sea turtles' first moments are the riskiest. After hatching on the beach, the youngsters dash toward the sea. Only a few escape the waiting gulls and other predators. Below, one sea turtle struggles with a crab while another makes it to the water.

sharks in the ocean. Fortunately, the female turtles lay a lot of eggs.

All green sea turtles lay their eggs the same way, whether in Panama or Pakistan. As the sun sets, the first female turtles slowly come ashore. In the water, these turtles can swim almost as fast as a grown man can run. But out on the sand, the 350-pound creatures crawl very slowly. By dark, however, the beach is alive with turtles. Some beaches have close to 1,000 turtles nesting at one time. Others have fewer than 50.

Turtles build nests, but not by pulling together sticks and grass the way some birds do. They dig deep holes to protect their eggs. A female first clears out a pit more than three feet long and a foot deep, about the size of her body. Resting in the pit, she then digs a small hole to hold her eggs.

Soon the eggs start to appear, coming out in small batches of one to four eggs at a time. When the female is finished, her nest will be filled with more than 100 eggs.

About two months later, the nests explode. At least it looks like an explosion, and that's what people call it. All the baby turtles in a nest hatch and pop out of the sand at one time. This happens at night or after a rainfall, when the sand is cool.

Scrambling wildly, the youngsters head right for the water. Even if they can't see the ocean, they usually head in the right direction. The sky is brighter over the water, and the turtles seem to know instinctively to head for the bright light. This is one of the most dangerous times in a green sea turtle's life. Hungry gulls, vultures, crabs, and other predators feast on many hatchlings as they cross the beach. Large fish may also snare them once they enter the water.

Where do young sea turtles go once they get to the sea? No one knows for sure. This is the so-called "lost year," when the small turtles drift with the currents. Some of them end up in drifting piles of sargassum weed. Ordinarily, the tangled weeds would be a safe hiding place for the youngsters. There the small turtles are out of sight of birds, sharks, and other enemies. But the currents

that bring sargassum weeds and sea turtles together also bring in polluting oil, plastic, and other debris. In the western Atlantic Ocean, many young green turtles have been found choked to death on globs of tar.

Scientists are learning where grown-up turtles go by putting tags on the females when they come ashore to nest. One group of nesting turtles was tagged on Ascension Island, halfway between South America and Africa. Later, those turtles were seen along the coast of Brazil, where they feed on sea grasses and algae. Getting from the island to Brazil was fairly easy. The turtles simply rode an ocean current that carried them there. Brazil was hard to miss, too, since its coastline stretches for more than 4,600 miles.

What still amazes scientists is how the turtles get from Brazil back to Ascension Island. The turtles cross 1,400 miles of open ocean and find a tiny spot of land barely seven miles across. That's like hiking from San Francisco, California, to Omaha, Nebraska, without using any maps. How do the turtles do it? Again, no one knows.

What is ahead for the green sea turtle? Scientists propose several ways to keep these animals from becoming extinct. First, enforce the laws that are already on the books. That means protecting the nesting beaches and controlling the harvesting of adult turtles in the sea. Some people recommend that no more turtle skins be taken to make leather, and that only poor people be allowed to catch the turtles for food. Companies should not be allowed to sell turtle soup and meat to nations that have other food supplies.

Some scientists are raising turtles to add to the supply in the wild. Turtle hatcheries raise green sea turtles from eggs brought in by local collectors.

One proposal, though, has turned out to be very controversial: raising these turtles for food. Some people believe that harvesting "home-grown" animals will take the pressure off the wild turtles. But others argue that poaching would get worse because the meat and soup sold by these farms would increase the world's demand for sea turtle products.

People are trying different ways to save sea turtles. In some countries, volunteers collect turtle eggs from the nests and hatch them in incubators. People then release the baby turtles on beaches (above) where they can scurry into the sea. In other places, people set up turtle farms (left) where they raise turtles for food. Harvesting only turtles from these farms takes the pressure off sea turtles in the wild. But some people worry that poachers will kill the wild creatures anyway.

You may have heard of many of the large endangered animals, like pandas and tigers and crocodiles, before you read this book. But many endangered animals are not so famous. The United States alone has more than 280 creatures on the list of endangered and threatened species. Large or small, each animal is special. If the species dies out, the animal is lost forever. On the next four pages, you can see some of the lesser-known endangered animals.

Lots of people don't like bats. But the endangered *gray bat* **(1)** is perfectly harmless and can even be helpful. It sleeps during the day and hunts at night. What does it eat? Lots of insects, including mosquitoes and other pests.

Smaller than pennies, the last of the many-legged *Socorro isopods* **(2)** live in the 90° F waters flowing from a single hot spring in New Mexico. Scientists want to study how these distant relatives of crabs and lobsters adapted to living in fresh water.

Not too many fish live in the desert. But one limestone pool in Death Valley, Nevada, is home of the *Devil's Hole pupfish* **(3)**. Unfortunately for the ¼-inch fish, the pool was partly drained to provide water for crops. Now, the area is protected and the species may survive.

The pretty shells of the *Oahu tree snails* **(4)** have been partly responsible for their disappearance. Some collectors boast of having more than 100,000 of the colorful shells in their collections. But every shell collected means one less living snail. By 1979, 22 of the original 41 species of these snails were extinct. The rest are endangered.

Hawaiian monk seals **(5)** are among the most endangered of all seals. Because they

AND THE LIST GOES ON...

6

have always lived on isolated islands, they have no fear of people or animals. This natural tameness made them easy targets for early explorers, who hunted them for their fur and meat.

The *Everglades kite* **(6)** eats only one kind of food—a small snail called an apple snail. The bird uses its curved beak to dig the snail meat out of the shell. But this picky eater has a problem. Apple snails have been scarce in recent years. Without enough to eat, fewer kites can survive.

The country's first butterfly preserve was created outside San Francisco to help save *Lange's metalmark butterfly* **(7)**.

The *Kentucky cave shrimp* **(8)** doesn't need eyes since it lives in dark underground streams. The endangered blind shrimp lives by eating decaying plants and bat droppings.

A toad may seem like a common animal, but this one isn't. The *Houston toad* **(9)** has been listed as an endangered species since 1970. Now, the state of Texas has created a park to help it survive.

IS THERE ANY HOPE?

The story of endangered animals sounds grim. We have already lost the dodo, Steller's sea cow, the passenger pigeon, the dusky seaside sparrow, and many more creatures. All the animals you've read about in this book are in danger of becoming extinct. Scientists think that as many as 10,000 animal and plant species become extinct every year. More creatures that we don't even know about may also be in trouble.

Fortunately, not every animal that is endangered becomes extinct. When people really try, they can come up with ways to rescue some of the endangered creatures.

Beautiful birds called snowy egrets and common egrets were saved more than 75 years ago. Both kinds of egret bred in the southern United States. They were killed for their delicate plumes, which were shipped to New York for decorating hats. By the early 1900s, only 18 common egrets were left in Florida. As a result, Florida passed a law protecting egrets and many other birds. Later, after a game warden protecting the egrets was killed by poachers, New York and other states passed laws banning the sale of all feathers taken from wild birds. The birds were finally out of danger. Today the egrets are a common sight throughout the South.

Animals have been saved in many other countries, too. In 1865, a French priest trav-

eling in China saw some unusual deer that were unknown in Europe. The deer had long tails and stood less than four feet high. The priest told scientists back home about the deer, and soon European zoos bought some from China. The animals were named Père David's deer, in honor of the priest, Père (Father) Armand David.

Having these deer safe in zoos later proved to be a blessing for the animals. Some of the deer in China were drowned in floods, and the rest were eaten by starving people during a famine. By 1921, the only Père David's deer left in the world were those in the European zoos.

Then a British nobleman, the Duke of Bedford, got together as many of the surviving deer as he could. He took them to his large estate in England. He wanted to breed them in captivity. His work succeeded, and in 1956 he had enough deer to send a small group back to China.

Saving animals is more than a story from the past. What people did years ago to save animals often works today, too.

State laws banning the sale of feathers from wild birds helped save the egrets. Today, a federal law protects hundreds of animals as well as plants. That law is the Endangered Species Act. It requires the government to list animals that are in danger of becoming extinct. Once identified, the endangered animals and their habitats are protected by the law. People cannot kill these animals, or buy and sell them, or own products made from their shells, fur, bones, or other parts of their bodies.

The Endangered Species Act also requires the government to identify animals that are threatened. Those animals are not endan-

Snowy egrets (left) and bison (inset) nearly became extinct less than 100 years ago. Bison were losing grazing lands to settlers, and both species were overhunted. At last the killing was outlawed, reserves were created for bison, and neither animal is endangered today.

gered, but they could be soon if steps are not taken to protect them and their habitats.

The list of endangered and threatened species has more than 880 names on it. More than 3,800 other species are under consideration for adding to the list. Each proposed species must be reviewed. Sometimes that takes several months. As a result, only about 60 species are added to the list each year. At that rate, it will take more than 60 years to study just the current candidates. At the same time, scientists are finding new species to add to the list each year.

Many nations around the world also support a treaty called CITES, the Convention of International Trade in Endangered Species. These countries agree not to sell endangered animals—or animal parts, such as horns and skins—to other countries. They also agree not to *buy* any endangered animal products.

Laws and treaties like these help if they are enforced. Enforcing the laws is difficult. In Mexico, armed soldiers sometimes guard beaches where sea turtles have nested. They want to keep poachers from stealing the eggs. In Africa, game wardens have had shoot-outs with poachers who try to kill endangered rhinos.

In the United States and other countries, customs agents watch to prevent products made from endangered animals from being brought into their countries. Some tourists don't realize that things made of Asian elephant ivory, Nile crocodile skin, polar bear fur, and sea turtle shell are banned.

Some smugglers have tried hiding endangered parrots inside car doors. Others have hidden small animals in secret compartments in boxes filled with poisonous snakes. One fur dealer labeled his boxes "mink," hoping that no one would open them and find the real fur: cheetah.

The Endangered Species Act and CITES have been a real help in conserving endangered plants and animals. Laws aren't enough, though, if not enough animals are left to protect or if their habitat has been destroyed. Père David's deer was saved because one person cared and because a few

of the animals had been kept and bred in zoos. Some zoos today have set up programs just for the purpose of breeding endangered animals. Sadly, there is not enough room in our zoos to save all endangered animals. At the very most, zoos might be able to breed 500 to 900 different species. That sounds like a lot, until you remember that thousands of kinds of creatures become extinct every year.

Right now, zoos aren't set up to take on hundreds of breeding projects. But a beginning has been made. The American Association of Zoological Parks and Aquariums has drawn up a list of more than three dozen endangered animals that zoos are ready to breed. The animals range from Andean condors and Chinese alligators to Puerto Rican crested toads and Siberian tigers.

One of the most successful breeding programs involves Brazil's golden lion tamarin. This colorful monkey is not much larger than a squirrel. Like many jungle animals, the tamarins were running out of places to live. Their homes were being cleared to make room for farms and towns. Scientists predicted the golden lion tamarin would probably be extinct by 1985.

For several years, people had tried to save the tamarins in zoos. Too often, the animals got sick and died without breeding. Others did have youngsters, but then ignored them. In the 1970s, a research team was put together by the National Zoo in Washington,

People help endangered animals by creating parks, like this reserve in India, where animals can live in safety. Some people, like this park officer holding an orphaned tiger cub, help by caring for individual creatures. People also help by not buying things made from endangered animals. The reptile-skin products at top left are all illegal.

D.C., to study these problems and to solve them—if possible.

The scientists first found that the tamarins had been getting the wrong kind of food. People had long thought that tamarins ate only plants. By putting together a diet that included crickets and mice as well as apples and bananas, the scientists helped make the tamarins healthier. The scientists also found that some tamarins were dying of birth defects. By repairing these defects with surgery and mating only healthy tamarins, more animals were saved that might have been lost.

One of the strangest discoveries was that many mother tamarins didn't really know how to take care of their youngsters. Some animals do this by instinct. Tamarins had to learn how. Scientists solved this problem by keeping tamarin families together in the zoo. The youngsters then learned how to take care of babies by helping their parents when more babies were born.

Within a few years, the National Zoo had 400 golden lion tamarins. It gave some to nearly 50 other zoos around the country. At the same time, only about 125 golden lion

tamarins were left in the wild. Luckily, some people in Brazil were really concerned about these animals. They convinced their government to set aside 12,000 acres of tamarin habitat as a wildlife reserve. The next step was to release zoo tamarins into the wild and see if they could survive and breed.

Golden lion tamarins were first taken from the National Zoo and other zoos to Brazil in 1983. At first, the animals were kept in an enclosed area where they could practice climbing trees and finding hidden food. They also had to learn to avoid predators and not to try to eat poisonous food. Before long, they were on their own. Then a second group of zoo tamarins was brought to Brazil and released, and other groups followed.

By 1986, the new animals had spread throughout most of the reserve and even into other forests nearby. Some mated with wild tamarins, and some mated with other tamarins from the zoos. But the results were the same: more babies were being born. People who live near the reserve are excited about the project. They are eager to keep the forest safe for all animals. Brazil's golden lion tamarins are on their way to being saved.

Efforts to save such creatures as tamarins, pandas, and lemurs are important. But saving one kind of animal at a time is slow work, and thousands of species are dying out every year.

The goal must be to save the animals' habitats. For example, just one square mile

The future is getting brighter for South America's golden lion tamarin. More and more of the animals are being raised in zoos and released into protected rain forests in Brazil. African elephants, like these being observed by park officers in a helicopter, are less secure. Poachers sometimes enter parks to kill the animals for their ivory.

of jungle may have several hundred kinds of trees—and untold kinds of insects and other creatures. If that small piece of land can be saved, these plants and animals may be saved with it.

The United States has created national parks and wildlife refuges where many endangered and threatened animals survive. For example, Everglades National Park is home to endangered bald eagles, Florida panthers, Cape Sable seaside sparrows, Everglades kites, loggerhead turtles, American crocodiles, and many other creatures. The Devil's Hole pupfish is protected in Death Valley National Monument, California. And without the protection of Aransas National Wildlife Refuge and Canada's Wood Buffalo National Park, whooping cranes would probably be extinct in the wild.

Wood Buffalo National Park, where such creatures as whooping cranes and bison live in safety, is the largest park in the world. It is twice as large as Massachusetts.

In South America, the nations of Brazil, Bolivia, Peru, Ecuador, and Venezuela have already set aside enough land to cover the state of Mississippi. In France, parts of a vast area of marshes and lagoons known as the Camargue have been turned into nature reserves. These reserves are home to flamingos, wild horses, and a wide variety of other animals and plants.

The African nation of Tanzania has turned nine percent of its land into parks and reserves. To equal that, the United States would have to set aside an area the size of California, Oregon, and Washington state. In Israel, a former kibbutz is now home to growing numbers of such oddly named mammals as the ibex, oryx, and onager.

Stories like these are repeated dozens of times in countries around the world. Mario A. Boza, president of Costa Rica's National Parks Foundation, pointed out in 1986 how important these efforts are: "The creation of national parks and reserves is the biggest achievement in wildlife conservation during the past 15 years." By saving places where animals live, we save the animals, too.

YOU CAN MAKE A DIFFERENCE!

The problems endangered species face are sometimes very complicated. You may feel there's not much you can do to help. But individuals and citizens' groups have done a lot to make a difference. First, here are some tips to help you avoid supporting the harmful trade of plants and animals:

1 Buy only traditional pets such as dogs, cats, and rabbits. Most wild animals have a difficult time adjusting to life in captivity. (For example, most reptiles and tropical fish soon die in captivity). Wild animals can transmit diseases to people and other animals. Animals from other countries can also harm native animals if they escape.

2 If you buy a pet bird, stick to captive-bred species such as budgies (parakeets), canaries, or cockatiels.

3 If you get to visit other countries, don't buy souvenirs made from sea turtles, spotted cats, or marine mammals. If these products are brought back into the United States, the items will be taken away from you and you may be fined.

4 If you like to garden, when you buy plants look for cactuses and other plants that appear "perfect"—it's likely that they were not taken from the wild. Wild plants usually have scars and insect damage.

5 Avoid buying products made from the skins of snakes and other reptiles. Avoid buying coral and ivory jewelry, too. It's hard to tell if the materials were taken legally.

Check with your local nature centers and conservation groups. They may have information about endangered species in your own area. They might also know of endangered species projects and other efforts you could help support. You might even be able to do some volunteer work for a local endangered species effort. Some groups allow you to "adopt" an endangered animal for a certain fee. "Adoptive parents" usually receive photos, progress reports, and other information about their animals.
    Here are some organizations that help:

Bat Conservation International (BCI)
P.O. Box 16203
Austin, TX 78716

BCI likes to tell people what bats are really like, and how useful the creatures are. Some of BCI's projects help endangered bats, such as gray bats, big-eared bats, and flying foxes.

The Center for Plant Conservation
125 Arborway
Jamaica Plain, MA 02130

Among other things, the Center grows rare plants and preserves their seeds for the future through its network of participating institutions.

HEART
Box 681231
Houston, TX 77268-1231

HEART distributes a video entitled "The Heartbreak Turtle." For several years, the King Oak Nature Club of Oak Creek Elementary School in Houston has worked hard to help the endangered Kemp's ridley sea turtle. Their project is called HEART (Help Endangered Animals—Ridley Turtles). For more information, contact HEART leader Carole Allen at the above address.

The International Crane Foundation
E-11376 Shady Lane Rd.
Baraboo, WI 53913-9778

Features an "adoption" program.

Friends of the Sea Otter
Box 221220
Carmel, CA 93922

Films are available for all ages.

Save the Manatee Club
500 N. Maitland Ave., Suite 200
Maitland, FL 32751

Features an "adoption" program.

Whale Adoption Project
634 N. Falmouth Hwy.
Box 388
N. Falmouth, MA 02556

Features an "adoption" program.

World Wildlife Fund (WWF)
1250 24th St., NW
Washington, DC 20037

WWF has several projects dealing with endangered species, such as the giant panda, jaguar, mountain gorilla, and endangered parrots. You can specify which project you want to support.

For more information about the laws protecting endangered and threatened species, write to the U.S. **Fish and Wildlife Service**, Division of Endangered Species and Habitat Conservation, Mail Stop 400, ARLSQ, Washington, DC 20240.

Adapted from *NatureScope: Endangered Species—Wild & Rare,* © 1988 by the National Wildlife Federation.

CREDITS

Cover: Sharon Cummings. back cover: Frans Lanting. I: Franz J. Camenzind. 2-3: Frans Lanting. 4-5: Phil Dotson/DPI.

GONE FOREVER? 6: illustration by Rudolph F. Zallinger; inset: Jeff Foott. 7 left: WWF/Gerald Cubitt; right: Jeff Foott. 8: Leighton Warren/courtesy of Blacker-Wood Library, McGill University. 9 top: Sullivan & Rogers/Bruce Coleman Inc.; middle: "Shooting Wild Pigeons in Iowa"/Bettmann Archive; bottom: National Park Service. 10 top left: Doug Perrine/DRK Photo; top right: Robert Holland/DRK Photo; bottom left: Tom Myers; bottom right: Tom and Pat Leeson. 11 left: John Chellman/Animals Animals; right: Randall Hyman.

GIANT PANDA. 12: WWF/Dr. J. MacKinnon. 13: Sharon Cummings. 14: Sharon Cummings. 15: Franz J. Camenzind.

WHOOPING CRANE. 16: Lynn M. Stone/Bruce Coleman Ltd.; inset: Tom Mangelsen.

HUMPBACK WHALE. 17: Patuxent Wildlife Research Center. 18: Jeff Foott; inset: Tom Mangelsen. 19: Tom Mangelsen. 20: The Kendall Whaling Museum, Kendall, Massachusetts. 21: Mark J. Ferrari/Center for Whale Studies. 22: both by Deborah A. Glockner-Ferrari/Center for Whale Studies. 23: Cynthia D'Vincent/Intersea Research. 24-25: illustration by Alton Langford.

BLACK-FOOTED FERRET. 26: LuRay Parker/Wyoming Game and Fish Department. 27: Tim W. Clark. 28: LuRay Parker/Wyoming Game and Fish Department; inset: Jeff Foott. 29: Franz J. Camenzind.

KOMODO DRAGON. 31 top: Alain Compost/Bruce Coleman Ltd.; bottom: Kenneth W. Fink/Bruce Coleman Inc.

TIGER. 32: Nancy Adams/EPI. 33: Alan and Sandy Carey. 34 top: Belinda Wright; bottom: Gunter Ziesler. 35: Rajesh Bedi. 36-37: illustration by Alton Langford.

SMALL CATS. 38: Kevin Schafer/Tom Stack and Assoc. 39: Rod Williams/Bruce Coleman Ltd. 40: Jean Paul Ferrero/Ardea London. 41: Tadaaki Imaizumi/Nature Productions, Tokyo.

CROCODILES. 42: Wolfgang Bayer. 43: Wolfgang Bayer. 44: Jerome J. Montague. 45: Jonathan Scott/Planet Earth Pictures.

GORILLA. 46: Karl Ammann/Bruce Coleman Inc. 47: Peter Veit/DRK Photo. 48: Michael Nichols/Magnum. 49: Nicholas Devore III/Bruce Coleman Inc.

PEREGRINE FALCON. 50: Wendy Shattil and Bob Rosinski/Tom Stack and Assoc. 51: Richard P. Smith. 52 top: Kennan Ward/DRK Photo; bottom: Frans Lanting. 53: Frans Lanting.

NUMBAT, WOMBAT, AND WALLABY. 54: John Cancalosi. 55: Babs and Bert Wells/Oxford Scientific Films. 56 top: John Everingham; bottom: WWF/Fredy Mercay. 57: Bert Wells/Oxford Scientific Films.

NENE GOOSE. 58: Stephen J. Krasemann/DRK Photo. 59 top: Greg Vaughn; bottom: William E. Ferguson. 60-61: illustration by Alton Langford.

LEMURS. 62: Frans Lanting. 63: Frans Lanting. 64: Frans Lanting. 65: Rod Williams/Bruce Coleman Ltd. 66-67: illustration by Alton Langford.

BLACK RHINO. 68: Anthony Bannister/Anthony Bannister Photo Library. 69: Karl Ammann. 70: Jonathan Scott/Planet Earth Pictures. 71: Jonathan Scott/Planet Earth Pictures. 72-73: illustration by Alton Langford.

MURIQUI. 74: Andrew Young. 75: Andrew Young. 76: Andrew Young. 77: Russell Mittermeier. 78-79: illustration by Alton Langford.

GREEN SEA TURTLE. 80: Howard Hall; inset: David Hughes/Bruce Coleman Inc. 81 left: George H. H. Huey; right: George H. H. Huey/Animals Animals. 83: both by Frans Lanting.

AND THE LIST GOES ON. 84-85, 86-87: illustrations by Alton Langford.

IS THERE ANY HOPE? 88: William J. Weber; inset: Frank Oberle. 90: Kevin Schafer/Tom Stack and Assoc. 91 top: Belinda Wright/DRK Photo; bottom: Stanley Breeden/DRK Photo. 92: Rod Williams/Bruce Coleman Ltd.; inset: Anthony Bannister/Animals Animals.

Library of Congress Cataloging-in-Publication Data

Endangered animals.

"A Ranger Rick book."
Summary: Examines a number of endangered species, including the giant panda, black rhino, and green sea turtle, and discusses what is being done to save them.
1. Endangered species—Juvenile literature. 2. Rare animals—Juvenile literature. [1. Rare animals. 2. Wildlife conservation] I. National Wildlife Federation. II. Ranger Rick.

QL83.E53 1989   591.52'9   89-12099
ISBN 0-945051-09-3
ISBN 0-945051-11-5 (lib. bdg.)

Staff for this Book

Howard Robinson
Editorial Director

Victor H. Waldrop
Project Editor and Writer

Donna Miller
Design Director

Debby Anker
*Illustrations Editor
and Writer*

Michele Morris
Research Editor and Writer

Eason Associates, Inc.
Design

Cei Richardson
Editorial Assistant

Vi Kirksey
Editorial Secretary

Paul Wirth
Quality Control

Margaret E. Wolf
Permissions Editor

National Wildlife Federation

Jay D. Hair
*President
and Chief Executive Officer*

William W. Howard Jr.
*Executive Vice President
and Chief Operating Officer*

Alric H. Clay
*Senior Vice President,
Administration*

Francis A. DiCicco
*Vice President, Financial
Affairs and Treasurer*

Lynn A. Greenwalt
*Vice President and Special
Assistant to the President for
International Affairs*

John W. Jensen
*Vice President,
Development*

S. Douglas Miller
*Vice President, Research
and Education*

Kenneth S. Modzelewski
*Vice President,
Promotional Activities*

Sharon L. Newsome
*Acting Vice President,
Resources Conservation*

Larry J. Schweiger
*Vice President, Affiliate and
Regional Programs*

Stephanie C. Sklar
*Vice President,
Public Affairs*

Robert D. Strohm
Vice President, Publications

Joel T. Thomas
*General Counsel
and Secretary*

Acknowledgments

The problems of endangered animals are being addressed by many people in universities, government agencies, zoos, and conservation organizations around the world. The information in this book came from a variety of publications produced by people whose first-hand experience with endangered animals brings those problems to life. We gratefully acknowledge special help provided by our scientific consultant, Dr. Michael H. Robinson, Director of the National Zoological Park, Washington, D.C. Dr. Robinson reviewed each chapter of the text and offered useful insight into what people around the world are doing to protect and restore the earth's troubled wildlife.

NATIONAL WILDLIFE FEDERATION
1400 Sixteenth Street, N.W., Washington, D.C. 20036-2266